FRANKIE FISH

AND THE SONIC SUITCASE

Frankie Fish and the Sonic Suitcase
published in 2017 by
Hardie Grant Egmont
Ground Floor, Building 1, 658 Church Street
Richmond, Victoria 3121, Australia
www.hardiegrantegmont.com.au

A CiP record for this title is available from the
National Library of Australia.

Text copyright © 2017 Peter Helliar
Illustration and design copyright © 2017 Hardie Grant Egmont

Illustration by Lesley Vamos
Design by Kristy Lund-White

Printed in Australia by McPherson's Printing Group, Maryborough,
Victoria, an accredited ISO AS/NZS 14001 Environmental
Management System printer.

1 3 5 7 9 10 8 6 4 2

MIX
Paper from
responsible sources
FSC® C001695

FRANKIE FiSH

AND THE SONIC SUITCASE

PETER HELLIAR

Art by
LESLEY VAMOS

hardie grant EGMONT

FOR MY THREE CHAMPIONS,
LIAM, AIDAN & OSCAR. FIND WHAT
YOU TRULY LOVE AND BUILD
YOUR LIFE AROUND IT.

A SHORT BIT BEFORE WE MEET
FRANKIE FISH

One morning, an old man with a hook for a hand parks his beloved blue car outside a bakery.

He shuffles inside to buy a loaf of bread, and then shuffles out again a few minutes later with a bag swinging gently off his hook. Huffing and puffing along the way, the old man stops to yell at a pigeon on the bonnet of his car. The pigeon makes a deposit from its feathery bottom, which makes the old man yell even more.

Grumbling about the mess, the old man opens the car door and climbs in. He puts on his seatbelt and checks his rear-view mirror. Satisfied, he starts the engine.

Then he drives his beloved blue car forward, **SMASHING** through the window of the bakery.

Nobody is hurt. The baker is stunned. The car is totalled.

The old man, now parked inside his local bakery under bricks and breads and tarts, is Alfie Fish, and this single event may change the history of the world.

Why? I hear you ask.

To find out, you'll have to read on . . .

CHAPTER 1

WHEN GOOD PRANKS TURN BAD. REALLY, EXTREMELY, VERY BAD.

Francis Fish was **EXCITED**. Make that **SUPER EXCITED**. He couldn't have been more excited than if his hands were made of chocolate.

For one thing, it was the final day of school for the term, which meant that he was about to have two glorious weeks away from St Monica's Primary.

Even better, in just one sleep he would be joining his best friend Drew Bird, and the entire Bird family, at their beach house for the holidays. That meant he wouldn't have to spend the holidays as he usually did, helping out at the family business, Fish Pest Control. It also meant he didn't have to see his sister Lou, professional saint and Mum and Dad's absolute favourite (an accusation strenuously denied by Ron and Tina Fish) for fourteen whole days.

WIN + WIN = DOUBLE WIN!

Francis was over the moon. He hadn't been on many holidays, because his parents were generally too busy to take them. And he'd *never* been on one with a best friend, on account of never having had a best friend before. But that had all changed when Drew Bird arrived at school last term.

After Miss Merryweather had introduced Drew to the class on his first day, she said (in a decision she would soon come to regret), 'You can sit in the spare seat next to Francis Fish.'

Drew walked over and plonked down next to Francis, grinning broadly. 'Hiya, Frankie Fish,' he said. 'I'm Drew. Drew Bird!'

For a moment, the world stopped. It was as if Francis had stepped into a sudden ray of warm sunlight. Because this is the thing: no-one had ever called Francis 'Frankie' before, let alone given him a nickname that wasn't making fun of his fishy surname – and he immediately *loved* it. Francis felt a grin spread across his face.

Right there and then, Francis – no, *Frankie* Fish would have swum to China and back for Drew Bird.

The two boys quickly discovered that they shared a lot more in common than animal-based surnames. They both loved watching *Doctor Who*, they were both world-class spitters, and they were both awesome at pranks.

Well, Frankie was *pretty good* at pranks. He'd once covered Saint Lou's pet turtle in Post-It Notes, and on her birthday he put fake dog poo on her pillow. Classic stuff. But Drew Bird was a next-level prank **KING**. The kind of king who could set off a fart bomb in the staffroom during lunchtime and walk away without a scratch – or a stench, for that matter. In the short time he'd known Drew, Frankie's pranking skills had come along in leaps and bounds.

Which leads us to another reason why Frankie was excited. Today, on the last day of term, he and Drew were going to play their biggest ever prank together – and it was going to be epic.

Their target was the end-of-term assembly, which usually had all the excitement of a snail at a zebra crossing and went just as slowly. Painfully. Slowly.

But today's assembly would **NOT** be like that. Nope. No way. Because at today's assembly, Frankie and Drew had a little surprise planned. While Principal Dawson was boring everyone into a coma (definitely medically possible),

Frankie and Drew were going to release a banner behind his head that read:

HAPPY HOLIDAYS SUCKERS!!

Gold. Absolute. Gold.

It was good clean fun and the culmination of many hours' work. Drew was such a prank perfectionist that he kept altering the details. Every time Frankie thought the prank was set, Drew would turn up at school with an excited gleam in his eye and say, 'There's been a change of plans, Frankie! I've thought of something even better.'

It was like Drew was a professional prankster, while for Frankie it was a hobby. In fact, Drew Bird had already mapped out his future career as a YouTube Viral Prankster, which was at odds with his parents' plan for him to become a chiropractor. (Gary Bird had a history of chronic neck pain.)

It was only yesterday that they'd finally settled on the exact wording for the banner. They had planned to paint it together during lunch but they ran out of time, so in the end Drew took the paper and paint home to do it there. Frankie's job was to organise the ropes that would unfurl the sign.

As he got ready for school, Frankie daydreamed about all the fun and adventures he and Drew would have together on their holiday. Playing cricket on the sand, camping on the foreshore and, of course, the pranks they would dream up. Frankie even had a brand-new boogie board from his birthday that he was dying to try out. **PLUS** Gary Bird had promised that they'd go to an island where you could actually *ride* dolphins.

Just one more sleep, thought Frankie happily

as he hid the ropes in the bottom of his school bag. *And then I'll go on the adventure of a lifetime!*

At least, that had been the plan ... until Frankie and Drew's epic prank threw everything out the window.

After handing over the ropes to Drew at the front gate, Frankie didn't see his best friend again all morning. It was only when he was filing into the end-of-term assembly, right behind class prefect Lisa Chadwick (whose perfect ponytail kept swinging into his eye), that Drew appeared.

'Hey,' whispered Drew, pulling Frankie by the arm. 'Come with me.'

'Francis Fish and Drew Bird! Where are you two going?' snapped Miss Merryweather.

Miss Merryweather was very crotchety at the moment. The rumour in the schoolyard said this was because she was busy organising her wedding to her boyfriend Mr Hedge (**AKA the Hedgehog**), the sports teacher. She'd planned the menu. She'd selected her wedding dress. She'd even chosen the cake toppers. The only thing she hadn't been able to arrange was a proposal from the Hedgehog.

Drew rebounded quicker than LeBron James. 'Mr Bourke asked us to help with the audio-visual equipment,' he said.

He said it *so* quickly and *so* confidently that Miss Merryweather believed him, even though this went against everything she knew about Drew Bird, which was: *Never trust Drew Bird.*

As everyone else found their seats, Frankie followed Drew around the side of the stage and up the back stairs, both of them giggling like hyenas on laughing gas. A hush came over the assembly hall as Principal Dawson took the microphone, kicking things off with a warning to the Mosley triplets not to do whatever it was they were doing.

Frankie and Drew got into their pre-arranged positions. Frankie took hold of the rope that ran all the way up to the ceiling. The other end was tied in a knot around a large steel knob on the ground, which was usually used to secure the background scenery for the school play. Rehearsals for next year's performance of the new school musical (*Dewey: Decimated*, written by the overzealous librarian Miss Davis) had yet to begin. Drew would be on the other side of the stage with an identical rope-knot-knob set-up.

'Remember, we have to let go of the ropes together when I say **NOW**,' Drew whispered.

Frankie grinned and gave him a solid thumbs up (although technically it was only one thumb).

Drew winked at Frankie before tiptoeing away, like a thief in the night, to the other side of the curtains. Frankie Fish could barely hide his excitement. If he'd been a real fish, his tail would have been flapping with unbridled joy.

The assembly started and it was the snooze-fest Frankie had predicted. Mr Dawson started by thanking the school groundskeeper, Mr Harris, for his years of service, and wishing him luck for his retirement.

Frankie, for one, was not sorry to see the groundskeeper go. Mr Harris had never forgiven him and Drew for the time they swapped the labels on the tubs of fertiliser and weed-killer in the storage shed just before the national 'Best School Grounds' competition was judged. Mr Harris had sworn loudly that he'd get them back one day.

'Sorry, Old Man Harris, but your time is up,' murmured Frankie, as Mr Dawson handed the groundskeeper a watch and ushered him off stage.

Mr Dawson then spent two minutes telling off the Mosley triplets for still doing what he'd told them to *stop* doing, and gave everyone a lecture on appropriate assembly behaviour.

Frankie could barely contain himself, yet General Bird *still* didn't give the signal. The assembly was going on for so long that Frankie started to worry they might miss out on school holidays.

Frankie craned his neck to catch Drew's eye. Drew signalled him to **HOLD**.

The Hedgehog was on stage now, going on about how proud he was of the hockey team for fighting out the year despite not winning a single game. Then he cleared his throat and hitched up his tracksuit pants.

'It's time to make a *special* end-of-term announcement,' he said, and paused for dramatic effect. He was about to announce the purchase of new hurdles and he wanted to milk it for all it was worth.

Just at that moment, with a smile as wide as a soccer goal without a goalie, Frankie saw Drew give the thumbs-up.

'*Now!*' he hissed.

With a rush of excitement Frankie Fish promptly yanked the rope. The knot slithered undone and the rope whizzed up to the ceiling.

And as the banner fell Frankie saw Drew mouthing something else at him. He couldn't be completely sure, but it looked like he was saying: *'There's been a change of plans ...'*

Frankie felt uneasy. *Uh-oh ... what has Drew done?*

Frankie watched, frozen to the spot, as the enormous banner unfurled right behind the Hedgehog, who was enjoying the suspense.

Just as he was about to launch into the hurdle news, there was a scream from the audience.

It was a loud and screechy scream, almost a squeal. Like a mouse was loose in the auditorium. A mouse with a machete.

From his position, Frankie could not see what was on the banner. He looked across the stage to see Drew Bird grinning from ear to ear as he made the signal for '*Let's bail!*' before disappearing out of view.

But Frankie wanted to know what was going on. There was another squeal, which sounded like it came from the same person, or the same machete-wielding rodent. Frankie, confused and increasingly nervous, poked his head around the curtain as the whispers in the auditorium became louder.

Everyone was staring at Miss Merryweather, who was running up the stage stairs, her hair falling loose from its bun, her face pink with joy. The girls cheered as Miss Merryweather flung herself upon a clearly baffled Hedgehog, and planted the biggest kiss of all time *right on his lips*. The boys laughed and made vomit gestures to each other, but they were clearly loving the mayhem of the moment.

Even the teachers were smiling and clapping, which made Frankie relax a little. Maybe he and Drew were in the clear. After all, anything that makes people cheer and laugh and smile has to be a good thing. Doesn't it?

Frankie slipped down from the stage and into the assembly hall, and the banner behind the Hedgehog slowly came into view. As soon as Frankie saw it, his brain sent an urgent message to his mouth.

This is bad, very bad ...

Miss Merryweather was still smooching a bewildered Hedgehog, but she took a break and leaned over to grab the microphone.

'I DO!!!' she yelled, with all the volume and passion of a teenager at a pop concert.

The Hedgehog could not have been more confused if you'd asked him to wash his hair with a banana. Then he finally looked up behind him and got the shock of his life.

In big bright letters, the banner read:

NANCY MERRY
WILL YOU

That was **NOT** the message Frankie and Drew had agreed upon.

Where was the **HAPPY?** Where was the **HOLIDAYS?** And where was the **SUCKERS???!!!**

Miss Merryweather was jumping up and down like she'd just won an all-expenses-paid trip around the world. The Hedgehog looked like he'd just found out he had to pay for it.

A beaming Principal Dawson took the microphone and said, 'Well, what a great start to the holidays. Have a great last day of term, everyone!'

As everyone showered the happy/confused couple with congratulations, Frankie realised he had to get away from the crime scene as quickly as possible. Maybe no-one had seen him pull that rope. Maybe if he laid low for the rest of the day, until the final bell rang ...

But just as he was slipping out the hall doors, a bony hand gripped his shoulder. Frankie turned to see Old Man Harris holding up an ancient video camera.

'I've had this set up and trained on the stage all morning to film my farewell,' he said triumphantly. 'And guess what else I've caught on tape? Two no-good pranksters! Fish Guts, you and your bird-brained buddy are in *so* much trouble.'

CHAPTER 2

OLD-PEOPLE JAIL

'I'm sorry, OK,' said Frankie from the back seat, as the Fish Pest Control mini-van pulled away from the school. 'I *said* I was sorry!'

'Well, you'll go on being sorry,' roared Ron Fish from the front, *'because you are grounded for **LIFE!***'

'*Life?*' said Frankie. 'What does *that* mean?'

'No TV, no iPad, and no computer either,' his dad continued bellowing. 'And if you think you're going to the beach with the Birds tomorrow, forget it! In fact, you're never going to see that Bird boy ever again!'

'**NEVER?**' Frankie bellowed back.

'NEVER! **NEVER! NEVER!**'

Ron Fish bellowed ever louder, as if he were the world-champion bellower reclaiming his championship. 'I've already spoken with Gary Bird, and he agrees. Your friendship is **DONE**.'

In an instant, Frankie's daydreams shattered. His first-ever holiday with a friend. Trying out his brand-new boogie board. Riding the dolphins. *Kaput, kaput, kaput.* He hadn't even had a chance to talk to Drew about what happened. Even when they'd been side-by-side in Mr Dawson's office, Drew had only been able to mutter a faint 'sorry, Frankie' before everyone started yelling at them.

'**THAT'S NOT FAIR!**' he cried.

Ron Fish pulled the car over to the side of the road, slammed on the brakes and turned around. 'Is it FAIR that your mother and I were

DRAGGED away from work because our SON reduced a teacher to TEARS? Is it fair that Miss Merryweather was humiliated in front of the ENTIRE SCHOOL? Is THAT fair, Francis? **IS IT?**'

Frankie crossed his arms and slumped down in his seat. OK, fine, it *wasn't* fair.

'Francis, you're only making it worse for yourself,' said a calm voice from the seat next to him.

That voice belonged to Saint Lou. She was two years older than Frankie, and super-smart, super-popular and super-well-behaved. This made Frankie resent her a little, and by a little I mean a *lot*. Especially right now.

'Don't you have anything to say in your defence?' demanded his mum Tina, also known as Tuna.

Yes, thought Frankie, sulkily. *It wasn't my idea to write that message.*

But he couldn't say that. He and Drew had a pranksters' code: they didn't rat each other out. Not ever. When Drew was blamed for the itching powder Frankie had sprinkled through every open car window in the staff carpark, he said nothing – even when he was put on yard duty for two weeks. And now, Frankie was honour-bound to do the same, no matter what the consequences.

At that moment, Frankie wished harder than

he'd ever wished for **ANYTHING** that his entire family would disappear so he could move in with the Birds and be happy forever.

'*Well, Francis?!*' his dad thundered again.

'He's probably in a state of shock after today,' Lou said. 'Maybe he's got PTSD or something. You know, like when soldiers come home from war.'

'If anyone has PS3 it's *you*, Lou,' Frankie snapped, not realising his sister was trying to help.

'Yeah, well he better get out of that state,' shouted their dad as he pulled back onto the road, 'before he gets to Grandad and Nanna's house!'

'**WHAT!?**' yelled Frankie. 'You can't send me there!'

'Francis, your father and I are very busy with the pest-control business,' said his mum. 'We just haven't got time to worry about you misbehaving –'

'No way,' said Frankie, shaking his head vigorously. 'I'm not going. That place is like **Old-People Jail**.'

'Well, I guess that'll make you its *youngest* prisoner!' said Ron Fish, glaring into the rearview mirror at Frankie, who looked like he'd just swallowed a fart. 'Because you'll be spending the whole school holidays there – starting **TOMORROW**.'

The following day, the Fish Pest Control minivan was as silent as a church service for mice. Frankie glared out the window as they drove. He hated visiting his grandparents. It wasn't just that it was boring, although it definitely was.

Nanna and Grandad, also known as Mavis and Alfie Fish, were basically living in the dark ages, with only one TV and no computers. The only vaguely modern thing in their whole house was Nanna's electric can-opener, which she thought was 'all a bit whiz-bang'. Frankie thought it might have been because they'd lived in Scotland before they came to Australia. Maybe people in Scotland didn't have the internet and computers and stuff like everyone else.

The real problem, in any case, was Grandad Alfie Fish: the grumpiest, sourest, meanest old man in the history of mean old men. He made Old Man Harris look like the Easter Bunny. Grandad barely spoke to anyone besides Nanna, preferring to spend almost all his time in the shed at the bottom of the garden, where no-one else was allowed to go.

It didn't help that Grandad had a hook instead of a right hand, which Frankie secretly thought was a bit creepy.

He knew he shouldn't, but he did. Annoyingly, nobody would tell him how Grandad had lost the hand in the first place. It was just never spoken about, like Miss Davis's moustache or Principal Dawson's nineties cover band, the Matchbox Blossoms.

So Frankie Fish was left to draw his own conclusions.

A. Grandad's hand was bitten off by a shark.

B. Grandad was actually **Luke Skywalker** in disguise.

C. Grandad had high-fived Edward Scissorhands and come off second-best.

Frankie had once *prayed* that it was B.

Frankie liked Nanna Fish OK, because she **LOVED** kids, had sparkly blue eyes and made good pancakes. But visiting Frankie's grandparents was like sitting down to a bowl of ice-cream when there's a plate of rotten meat beside you. Sure, ice-cream is nice, but it's hard to enjoy when there's the stench of putrid flesh in your nostrils.

Frankie's mum turned around from the front seat of the car. 'You know your grandad lost his driver's licence recently,' she said. 'You can help your grandparents out by running errands. They could really use an extra hand around the place.'

At any other time, Frankie might have laughed at the accidental joke, but today he couldn't even muster a smirk. His not-a-smirk soon drooped even lower as the Fish family's mini-van pulled into the long driveway.

They'd arrived at Old-People Jail.

'Dad, I'm sorry, OK?' Frankie said desperately,

trying to sound EXTRA sorry. 'You've made your point. Now let's go home.'

But Ron Fish just gave Frankie a look, and then honked twice.

'Be good, Francis,' said his mum, giving him a squeeze.

Saint Lou gave her brother a sympathetic look, which Frankie misinterpreted to mean, 'Suck eggs, loser!'

'Aren't you coming in?' he said to his family, trying to keep a wobble out of his voice. Maybe if they were reminded how boring it was at Nanna and Grandad's, they'd realise this was a ridiculously big punishment. Maybe he'd even be allowed to go away with Drew after all. Or at least be able to *call* him.

But Tina and Ron weren't falling for that. 'Help Nanna around the house,' his mum said, 'and stay out of Grandad's way. And remember, **DO NOT** go near his shed.'

A moment later, Frankie was left standing in

the driveway as his family's mini-van screeched off like they'd just robbed a bank – taking his dreams with them.

CHAPTER 3

A MOMENT OF
MADNESS iN A
MAD, MAD PLACE

Five minutes later, Frankie sat down on Nanna's couch with his boogie board (which he'd brought just in case). His jail sentence felt super harsh, especially when he thought of all the fun he *should've* been having at the beach. He tried very hard not to cry, and bravely succeeded.

Frankie could hear Nanna humming in the kitchen as she prepared morning tea.

Grandad was sitting in his armchair with a newspaper open in front of him. He turned a page, ignoring Frankie completely.

Frankie stared at Grandad for a moment, and then at the painting above his head. It was of dogs playing poker, and had hung on that wall for as long as Frankie could remember. He didn't find it particularly funny but perhaps Grandad did.

'Dogs playing poker,' he said meekly. 'Classic.'

Grandad didn't even move his head to acknowledge the comment.

After another long silence, Frankie decided to start again. 'Um, hi, Grandad,' he tried. 'What's in the news today? Anything good?'

Silence. Grandad turned another page.

'Did you know you can read a newspaper on a computer these days? That might be easier on your hook because, um, you don't have to turn pages on a computer,' Frankie went on politely. 'Yeah, we all use computers now. Do you even know what a computer is?'

More silence. A frown deepened across Grandad's forehead.

Frankie cleared his throat. It occurred to him that it'd been a while since he'd seen his grandad, and it was possible that he'd gone deaf since then. Frankie increased the volume.

'Grandad? I said -'

Suddenly, Grandad stood up and glared at Frankie. Then he scrunched up his newspaper and slammed it on the table – which would have been very dramatic and scary, except that several of the pages got stuck on Grandad's hook, and he had to wave the hook around wildly to get them off while the sports section flapped about like a pelican in a bathtub.

Frankie froze, not even daring to snicker.

Grandad finally freed the crumpled newspaper from his hook, banged it on the table and stomped out of the room. A moment later, Frankie heard the back door slam. Without even noticing, he let go of his boogie board, which was fast becoming the saddest boogie board in the world.

So began Frankie's school holidays.

The one good thing about his grandparents' house was that it was clean and smelt nice (no thanks to Grandad Fish Guts). The floors were regularly mopped, the polka-dot curtains framed spotless windows and the aroma of blueberry pancakes wafted through the air.

Another plus was that Grandad, Captain Hook, spent most of his time in his shed. But it was frustrating that no-one else was ever allowed to take so much as a peek inside.

What if you were being attacked by zombies? '**NO**. Stay out of Grandad's shed.'

What if you were being attacked by zombies with axes and guns and girl germs? 'NO. Stay out of Grandad's shed.'

What if you desperately needed to do a poo and the last roll of toilet paper in the whole world was in Grandad's shed? 'NO. Find a news-paper and STAY OUT OF GRANDAD'S SHED.'

Of course, being forbidden just made Frankie more curious than ever.

'What does Grandad do all day in that shed?' he asked Nanna as she brought over a bag of marbles.

'I'm not really sure, dear,' admitted Nanna. 'He tinkers mostly, I think. Whatever it is, it keeps him busy and out of my hair.' She winked as Frankie's eyes darted up to her purple hairdo.

Nanna didn't seem to mind keeping *Frankie* in her hair, though. Which was lucky, because it wasn't like there was anywhere else he could go. There was nothing for Frankie to do but play marbles, listen to talkback radio, and watch game shows on the little TV that Nanna loved so much. Sometimes he laid his boogie board on the lounge carpet and tried to pretend he was riding a dolphin at the beach with Drew Bird.

Nights overtook mornings and mornings overtook nights as Frankie's sentence ticked away, and one thing remained the same: he was **BORED** out of his **BRAIN**. And then late one afternoon, just as Nanna sat down with a cup of tea for another episode of *Family Feud*, Frankie decided enough was enough.

He sneaked into the hallway and picked up the ancient landline.

A chirpy Ron Fish answered the phone. 'Fish Pest Control! If there is a pest, we'll do the –'

'Hi, Dad. It's me, Frankie.'

'Frankie?'

'Yeah, your son?'

'Hey, Francis,' Ron said, sounding more normal. 'How are you enjoying Nanna's?'

Frankie took a deep breath. 'Look, I was just

wondering if I could come home,' he said politely. 'I've been here for a very, very long time now –'

His dad groaned loudly. *So much for customer service*, thought Frankie.

'Mate, it's been *forty-eight hours*,' his dad said. 'Don't call us at work unless it's an emergency, OK? We need to keep the line free. Your mother will come get you when we're ready.'

Click. The phone went dead, and so too did Frankie Fish's hopes of early release.

Frankie dragged himself back into the lounge as the Murphy family on the TV tried to think of another thing you might do with a zucchini.

'*Erm ... use it to clean your ear?*' suggested Mrs Murphy.

Frankie slumped onto the coffee table, feeling the weight of his sentence on his shoulders. Near his head was a little vase of blue flowers. He stared at it glumly.

Nanna's bright eyes twinkled as she looked at him. 'Do you know what those flowers are called?' she asked, turning down *Family Feud* for a moment.

Frankie shrugged. 'Blue roses?'

'*Myosotis sylvaticas,*' Nanna Fish said.

'Oh yeah, that was my next guess,' replied Frankie sheepishly.

Nanna plucked a single flower from the vase. 'Otherwise known as forget-me-nots,' she said, popping it in Frankie's shirt pocket.

'Um, thanks,' Frankie replied, not sure what he was going to do with a flower. Then, just to make conversation, and even though he knew the answer already, he said, 'Where's Grandad?'

Nanna looked at Frankie, a smile tugging at her lips. 'In the shed, most likely.' Then she sighed. 'He's been spending a lot more time in there lately. He's been a little grumpy, too. Have you noticed that?'

'Um,' said Frankie. He *wanted* to say that Grandad was never *not* grumpy, but he didn't want to hurt Nanna's feelings. 'Not really,' he said carefully. 'He seems the same as always.'

Nanna closed her eyes for a moment. 'Losing his driver's licence was a big deal for your grandad,' she said quietly. 'He's loved driving his whole life, even after the terrible accident that cost him his hand ...'

Frankie held his breath. Could *this* be the moment when he finally found out what happened to Grandad's hand? Not even Saint Lou knew that. Frankie would have bragging rights forever. 'What accident?' Frankie asked, not wanting to sound too keen. 'Has he crashed into other bakeries before? Or was it ... a butcher's?' Nanna shook her head. 'You will never guess,' she said. 'Not in a **MILLION** years.'

'Was Grandad a pirate?' Frankie guessed enthusiastically. 'Was he made to walk the plank and had his hand eaten by a crocodile?'

Best. Theory. Ever.

But then Nanna looked at the clock on the wall and said exactly what Frankie was hoping she wouldn't say. 'Oops, it's late – I've got to serve up dinner.'

She gave Frankie another bright smile, though he thought her eyes looked a little moist. 'You go tell Grandad to his *face* that if he isn't sitting at this table in thirty seconds, he's not having any dinner at all.'

'But he's in his shed,' protested Frankie. 'I'm not allowed in there!'

'Just knock and call out his name then – that should do it.'

'Okaaaay,' Frankie said, unconvinced.

He headed outside, past the roses and daffodils, through Nanna's beautiful garden, which truly was like Disneyland for bees. He walked past the sunflowers and the forget-me-nots, down the brick path to the shed. He felt like a golden retriever, but instead of retrieving a tennis ball he had to bring back a cantankerous, crusty old man. A tennis ball would have been way more fun and much less angry.

The back of the garden seemed dark and ominous, though that was maybe just the shade of the leafy maple tree hanging overhead. With every step Frankie's feet grew heavier.

He arrived at the shed door with his palms sweaty and his heart beating. Frankie had never been within two metres of the shed before, so it felt like a historic moment. If he'd had his dad's iPhone with him, he would have taken a quick selfie to mark the occasion.

KNOCK KNOCK!

'Grandad-Nanna-said-if-you-don't-come-now-you-won't-get-any-dinner.'

He said it quickly, ready to run if the old man yelled at him.

No response. Frankie repeated himself, this time louder and slower. Still nothing.

Frankie felt himself get a little bolder. He banged on the door a few times. 'Grandad, Nanna said if you don't come now, she'll let the neighbours' cat wee in your cornflakes.'

Nothing. He thumped the shed door. Hard.

'Grandad, Nanna said if you don't come now, she'll wash all your clothes in gravy and then roll them in seeds so you get attacked by pigeons on your morning walk!' Frankie yelled at a volume that could be heard four blocks away.

Nothing again.

Frankie was really annoyed now. He hated being ignored by the kids at school, and he hated being ignored at home even more – but at this moment, there was nothing worse than being completely ignored by Grandad.

'**GRANDAD!!!**' Frankie yelled, and then, in a moment of utter madness, going against everything he knew to be good and wise and holy, he pushed open the door and stomped **INSIDE** the forbidden shed.

CHAPTER 4

THE SHED OF
SECRETS

Frankie was breathing heavily, his shoulders bobbing up and down like beach balls lost at sea. He couldn't believe that he was actually inside the totally-out-of-bounds, not-even-in-a-zombie-apocalypse shed ... but where was Grandad?

Frankie gulped as he hung nervously near the doorway. 'Grandad?' he said softly, just in case the old crank was hiding.

He knew he should probably get out of there, but this was a once-in-a-lifetime opportunity – like kicking the winning goal at the World Cup or eating ice-cream for breakfast. So Frankie decided to take a sneaky peek around. He felt like Neil Armstrong arriving on the moon: one small step for Frankie Fish, and one huge leap for Fish-kind.

Inside, the shed was dark and dusty. Frankie crept in stealthily, like he was attempting to steal jewels from around the Queen's neck while she slept. The dusty floorboards creaked under his feet, and with every sound his heart raced a little faster. In the centre of the shed he stopped and waited impatiently as his eyes adjusted to the gloom. Finally he would get to see what his grandfather kept hidden in here!

Hmm ... Spare parts from dishwashers and car engines adorned the benches, alongside jars brimming with rusty screws.

Frankie sighed. **Total. Bummer.**

This was the biggest anti-climax since the top deck of the Double-Decker Bus was ruled out-of-bounds on the Double-Decker Bus excursion because of Miss Merryweather's fear of heights. Taking a deep breath, Frankie sneaked even deeper into the shed. Maybe the good stuff was right at the back.

But there were no moon craters or alien life forms to be seen, just wonky shelves lined with dusty trophies, frayed ribbons and faded certificates, as well as some dog-eared black-and-white photos of a car race.

Frankie leaned closer to examine the blown-up photograph of a dashing young driver. He was leaning against a number 42 racing car, looking cheerful and strangely familiar. Squinting, Frankie read the faded lettering in the photo's white border: *Alfie Fish. Glasgow 1952.*

WHAT. THE?!

The blond bombshell next to the racecar was Frankie's own grandad! He looked so different.

Fit and healthy and weirdest of all ... happy. A strange feeling burbled inside Frankie Fish. This guy was *cool*.

In another photo, Alfie held up a huge trophy as two smiling women in stiff, old-fashioned dresses poured a bottle of champagne over him. Frankie knew that if he tried that, he'd be in big trouble – but in the photo Alfie was beaming.

At the back of yet another shelf was a photo of an older man in a trench coat leaning into young Alfie's racecar. The writing on the border said: *Ernest gives me last minute instructions.*

Frankie wasn't exactly an expert on the Fish family tree, but he knew his great-grandparents' names were Ernest and Edna. He examined the image closely. Ernest had hands the size of Christmas hams and a smile as wonky as a day-old donkey. Behind the car was another figure – a boy who looked a lot like Alfie, only smaller. Could this be his grandad's mysterious brother, the one no-one ever spoke about?

Frankie scratched his forehead. Was he called Robbie? Ronnie? No, Roddy – that was it. Roddy was staring at Alfie like he thought he was the greatest person ever, but Alfie was paying him no attention. *I know how that feels*, thought Frankie bitterly.

Returning the photo to the shelf, Frankie caught sight of something yellow sticking out of a book. Carefully, he took the book off the shelf – *Gravitational Space: The Mechanics of Time Travel*, it said on the cover – and removed two delicate pieces of paper.

The first was a newspaper clipping, headed:

BIG RACE ENDS IN BIG TRAGEDY

Frankie read aloud to himself:

One thing is certain: the championship of 1952 will be remembered not for reigning champion Clancy Fairplay taking the chequered flag, but for race leader Alfie Fish skidding through an oil mark on the final turn and tragically crashing. Reports are emerging that it has cost him his right hand – and maybe even ended his boyhood dream.

Right there and then, you could have knocked Frankie down with three quarters of a feather. Without even meaning to, he'd solved the mystery of the missing hand. Frankie's eyes were drawn back to the image of young Alfie proudly clutching the trophy.

Poor Grandad, thought Frankie.

The other piece of paper was just an old advertising flyer, depicting a man with a pencil-thin moustache and a cape, hand-drawn in black ink. **THE AMAZING FREIDO**, with his fierce stare and dramatic hand gestures, seemed to be summoning words that appeared in puffs of smoke.

The artist had drawn electrical bolts flying in and out of a wonky-looking cube.

It was the kind of cheesy old thing that Frankie was sure Drew would get a big kick out of. He slipped it in his pocket, next to the forgotten forget-me-not. When – *if* – he ever got to see his friend again, he'd show it to him.

THE AMAZING FREIDO
A LADY SAWN IN HALF!
ANIMALS APPEAR OUT OF THIN AIR
PLUS....
SIX ELECTRIC EELS & THE WATER TANK OF DEATH!

It was only when Frankie was about to leave the shed that he noticed the ruby-coloured suitcase sitting open on an adjacent bench.

Usually, a suitcase on a bench in a shed wouldn't be of much interest – but considering the startling developments of the past few minutes, Frankie sensed that it might not be your regular, run-of-the-mill suitcase.

Frankie edged closer and peered in. He wasn't sure what he was expecting to see – spare hand-hooks, maybe? – but he definitely *wasn't* expecting a computer. Well, a sort of computer. It was a hybrid of an old chunky laptop and a typewriter, connected with hundreds of tiny wires and held together with occy straps.

Unbelievable, thought Frankie, as all the sympathy he'd been feeling melted away. *He's been secretly using a computer this whole time! Could he BE any more selfish?*

He took a closer look. The computer, if it could be called that, had a small screen set into the lid. The suitcase itself was quite impressive, with a leather handle, a hard case and tiny monograms that Frankie could only just make out as 'HT'.

There was a soft whispering noise behind him and Frankie whipped around, his heart beating madly. But no-one was there.

He knew Grandad could come back any minute. If Frankie was going to snoop around, he'd better hurry – and the main thing was to find out if this computer had internet access. Maybe he could get a message to Drew Bird.

Frankie went to press **ENTER** on the DIY keyboard, but something very strange happened. His finger went straight through the button and hit the wooden bench. It was only now that Frankie noticed the computer appeared to be shimmering slightly in the dusky light.

A message popped up on the screen in blinking green letters. *'The Time Computer is temporarily inactive as operation remains in progress.'*

Frankie frowned, sure he was being tricked somehow. It was bad enough that Grandad was a jerk, but for him to be a jerk who was playing a prank on Frankie – that was too much. Frankie and Drew were the prank kings, and nobody pranked the prank kings!

Two can play at this game, old man, thought Frankie. Nanna Fish wouldn't like Grandad disappearing around dinnertime, not one bit.

Carefully closing the shed door behind him, Frankie hurried down the brick path towards the house. He was so keen to dob on Grandad that he failed to notice the pretty flowers that had been growing in Nanna's garden were now weeds. If Frankie had been paying more attention, he'd have also noticed grasshoppers the size of soft-drink cans were hopping around where the forget-me-nots were only minutes earlier.

'Nanna!' Frankie yelled as he burst into the kitchen. 'I can't find Grandad. I think he's fled the country!'

But there was no sign of Nanna. Not only that, but the house had completely changed. It was as if Nanna had never lived there at all.

Now Frankie Fish was paying attention.

CHAPTER 5

THE MYSTERIOUS DISAPPEARANCE
OF NANNA FISH

Frankie did a double-take. He *had* walked into Nanna Fish's house, hadn't he? Yes, of course he had. The brick path he had danced down was the same, and the back entrance had the same flywire screen door – except now it had a hole in it and was acting as a revolving door for flies and mosquitoes. It was the very same house in which he'd spent the last few days lying around in utter boredom. But it also wasn't.

'**Nanna!**' he called, darting from room to room.

But Nanna was nowhere to be found. There wasn't any trace of her. In the lounge room, Nanna's bright polka-dot curtains had been replaced by a wrinkled brown pair that were drawn tightly closed, even though it was still light outside. The scent of home-cooking had gone, and a stale funk lingered instead, as if the windows had never been opened. Beneath Frankie's sneakers, Nanna's freshly mopped floors were now crusted with a thick layer of old dirt.

Frankie started to feel a bit scared. 'What's going on?' he said aloud to the dark house.

He hurried to the phone. His dad had told him only to call home in an emergency. But surely a missing Nanna and a weirdly different house qualified as one?

Riiiiiing, ring.
Riiiiiing, ring. Riiing -

A bored-sounding man answered. 'Hello, this is Max's Fish-n-Chips. If you need dinner, we've got a –'

'Hello, is Tuna Fish there?' asked Frankie, his voice quivering.

'Ha ha, very funny,' the unfamiliar man said. 'Are you just making a prank call or do you want some fish and chips?'

'D-dad?' Frankie said, almost whispering.

The man snorted and hung up. Frankie put down the phone, his hand trembling. What was happening?

'Mavis. Mavis!'

It was Grandad bellowing from outside – and for the first time ever, Frankie was relieved to hear it. The back door swung open, and

Grandad's voice became louder and more urgent.

'Mavis!'

Frankie walked into the grimy kitchen, feeling as though his feet were on backwards. A flustered-looking Grandad was standing there, gaping at the funky smell, the darkness, the ugly curtains – the very changes that Frankie had gaped at too.

A small part of Frankie was relieved that someone else was seeing this too, and he wasn't going crazy. But a much *larger* part of him wished that the 'someone else' was anyone but his grandad.

'Mavis?' Grandad said again, more worried this time. He finally noticed Frankie, and for once he didn't glare. 'Have you seen Nanna?'

'She's not ... here,' Frankie said numbly. 'Grandad, *what's going on?*'

But Grandad just stood there, terror written all over his face. 'Oh dear Lord,' he whispered.

Frankie was properly scared now. 'Please,

Grandad,' he said. 'Nanna's gone, and then I tried to call my parents, but the phone number is different, and –'

Suddenly Frankie remembered the peculiar computer in the suitcase, and the message saying *operation remains in progress*.

The hairs on Frankie's neck stood up like the national anthem was being played. 'Did you *do* something to Nanna? Did you make her go away?'

'How *dare* you accuse me!' spat Grandad. But he looked guilty.

Something shifted inside Frankie. He went from feeling scared to **ANGRY**. Grandad had obviously done something to Nanna, maybe even erased her. As Miss Merryweather would say, it warranted a rise in tone.

'This has something to do with that dumb computer in your shed, doesn't it?' Frankie said, his voice loud and strangely high. 'I saw it, Grandad. And I know something weird is going on!'

'Been snooping in my shed, have you?' roared
Grandad. 'Not another word from you, boy.
Just *stop*!' he snapped, and thrust his hand in
front of him like a police officer directing traffic.
And indeed Frankie *did* stop. But not because
his grandad had ordered him to – no,
Frankie was beyond listening

to the old man's orders at this point. It was because the hand Grandad was holding up was ... his **right hand**.

Alfie Fish's right hand, which had been missing for more than fifty years, was back.

Frankie went back to being scared again. 'Wh-wh-what – where's your hook?' he stuttered.

'You need to be **QUIET** and let me **THINK**,' Grandad said, running his hands through his thinning hair. 'Just shut your –'

'Wh-wh-what have you done?' Frankie pleaded. 'Why is everything suddenly different? *Where is* **NANNA FISH** *and* **YOUR HOOK** *and* **MY PARENTS?**'

Alfie Fish was clearly about to unleash another verbal barrage on Frankie when he suddenly stopped himself, lowered his hands and took a step closer to his grandson.

In a very different tone, he said, 'Oh my – your *face*,' and inspected every inch of Frankie's face as if he was trying to spot spinach between his teeth ... and up his nose and in his ears. He leaned back to pull open the curtains wider and let the fading evening light spill into the kitchen, and then stared at Frankie again. 'Your *face*,' he repeated with concern.

'My face? What about *your* face?' Frankie said defensively. 'It's old and wrinkly and –'

'Never mind,' muttered Grandad to himself. 'I need to go back.'

'Go *where?*' asked Frankie.

'Never mind.'

'Never mind? I *do* mind!' yelled Frankie.

'You're just a kid!' Grandad shot back. 'You don't know *what* you're dealing with.'

At that, Frankie lost it.

'And you're just a **CRAZY**, **MEAN** **OLD MAN** who's somehow **MESSED UP** **EVERYTHING** and made Nanna Fish **DISAPPEAR** and turned my family into a fish-n-chip shop, so wherever it is you're going, old man, **I AM COMING TOO!**' he screamed at the top of his lungs.

There was a very long pause that, if it had gone on any longer, could have asked for its own spot on the calendar. Frankie braced for impact.

Grandad grabbed Frankie by the arm, dragged him out of the kitchen, through the back door and down the back garden path.

Frankie barely had time to ask, 'Where are we going?' before he was back inside the Forbidden Shed (which appeared to be less and less forbidden by the minute) with the door slammed shut behind him.

CHAPTER 6

THE
WORST COMPUTER
IN THE WORLD

The mysterious old ruby suitcase was still open on the bench, but this time it wasn't shimmering. It looked solid, like it was actually on the wooden benchtop.

'Take a seat, boy,' said Grandad. 'We don't have much time.'

Grandad sat down heavily in an old chair and began furiously scribbling numbers on a bit of paper. Frankie just stared.

His grandad had *never* invited him to sit down with him, *ever*, let alone in this dusty forbidden shed. Frankie couldn't help but feel deeply weirded out by that on top of everything else.

Alfie glanced up at Frankie and frowned. 'Sit down *now!*' he barked.

Frankie did so hastily. Grandad jotted down a few more numbers before turning to the ruby suitcase and typing the numbers into the computer with his two index fingers. It began beeping softly.

'What are you doing?' croaked Frankie.

'Entering co-ordinates,' Grandad replied bluntly.

'What for? Is it Google Maps?' asked Frankie. 'Because you know you can just type in the address –?'

'This isn't the time for questions, boy,' snapped Grandad.

'I think it's exactly the time for questions,' Frankie snapped back, 'because if I don't ask questions, how the hell am I going to get answers? Tell me what you're doing on that damn computer!'

Frankie knew full well that he wasn't allowed to say 'hell' and 'damn', but this was an emergency (and also he liked the way it sounded). Grandad didn't tell him off, either. Instead, he took a very deep, long breath.

'Fine,' Grandad said with forced calm. 'But this isn't a computer, exactly. It's – it's – well, I would probably say something like it's a prototype device for manipulating spacial and chronological velocity and relative dimensional placement.'

'Huh?' said Frankie. It occurred to him that maybe Grandad hadn't taken his medication that morning.

Alfie Fish sighed again, and leaned in close to his grandson. When he spoke, his voice was a mix of frustration, anguish and … pride. 'It's a **TIME MACHINE**, Francis,' he said. 'It's a one-of-a-kind, wondrous time-travelling machine. And it *works*.'

Frankie leaned back as far as he could without falling off his chair. He was now completely certain that his grandad was off his old-man medication. 'Um, so ... where's Nanna?'

'Well, that's just it, boy,' Grandad blurted out, and his eyes filled with tears. 'I went back in time to fix a mistake and I think that might have made her disappear.'

The computer's quiet beeping suddenly stopped, then started again, louder and more insistent. Almost like a countdown.

'Grandad,' said Frankie nervously, 'why does that thing sound like Dad reversing out of the driveway?'

'Because we are going to get your nanna back,' said Grandad.

The beeps got even louder.

'But *how*?' said Frankie.

'Just think of it as reversing down a really,

really long driveway,' replied Grandad. 'Now, hold on and don't let go, whatever you do.'

Gulping, Frankie latched on to the suitcase handles and squeezed his eyes shut tight as Grandad typed one more thing into the old computer. 'Happy travels,' Frankie heard him mutter.

Then there was a blinding flash of light and Frankie's world turned upside down.

Imagine being stretched. Not just the kind of stretch you do after you've been sleeping in a weird position to get rid of the pins and needles and creaks in your bones.

No, imagine being stretched over time and space. Stretched like a rubber band to breaking point, or one of those elastic toys you get in lolly bags at a birthday party. Stretched like your skin is made of cheese on the world's cheesiest pizza.

Then imagine that as you're being stretched over time and space, the world is rotating beneath you and around you and flinging you through history in a big mishmash of colours and shapes, while your head is going in one direction and your brain is flung in the other. A million voices speak a thousand languages while the Statue of Liberty tumbles into the Pyramids and Genghis Khan rides a skateboard down a road made of stardust, alongside Roman Generals in their chariots being pulled by velociraptors.

This is what was happening to Frankie Fish and his grandad. Frankie could hardly tell what was real and what was not, let alone where his hands were and whether he still had knees. It was impossible to know *anything*, not even how long it lasted as they were catapulted through wormholes and time warps.

At one point, Frankie looked up and saw Grandad looking at him. The old man's words came out like a movie on the wrong speed.

'Geeeeeeet reaaaaaaaady.'

Then Frankie noticed the world spinning faster and faster around him, the voices getting louder, and somehow he could feel trees falling and rockets exploding and black clouds rumbling like a giant storm was imminent. Before he knew it, an exact moment in time and space had sucked Frankie and Alfie Fish into its belly like a vacuum sucking up ants.

This is so random, thought Frankie.

But it wasn't random at all.

It was time travel.

CHAPTER 7

SOME OTHER TIME

Grey clouds, wet grass and cold, fresh air.

That is what Frankie Fish saw, smelt and felt as he opened his eyes. Gone was the kaleidoscope of colours and the sounds of a million voices, replaced with a whistling cold and bitter wind.

'What just happened?' Frankie said groggily, feeling like he'd had a go on the world's worst roller-coaster ride.

He rubbed his eyes and looked around. He was in a paddock with grass as green as your greenest pencil, with enormous rocky boulders rising up from the ground.

Frankie blinked a few times, as if it might refresh the image in front of him. Still green. Still rocky.

Then he realised that on top of that, he was alone.

'Oh, no,' he groaned. 'Where's Grandad?'

Next moment, he heard a moan and a rumble from behind a large boulder nearby. Frankie got to his feet and soon found Grandad snoring with his mouth wide open, as happy as a pig in suspiciously stinky mud. Somehow, he was still gripping the ruby suitcase. Frankie bent down and said right into his ear: 'Grandad, are you OK?'

Grandad sat bolt upright. 'What time is it?' he demanded.

Frankie shrugged. 'I have *no* idea. I don't even

know if my butt's on the right way.'

Grandad leapt to his feet and started scanning the field, his eyes bright and clear. 'Bugger it, this isn't where I landed last time. We need to keep moving. The train will be approaching any minute and we can't miss it.'

Frankie raised an eyebrow. '*What* train? We're in the middle of nowhere.'

'Come on, boy – time travel waits for no man, nor his annoying grandson,' Grandad snapped like a piranha at a buffet before marching off.

'Hang on a second,' said Frankie, heart pounding with excitement. 'Are you telling me we just time-travelled?'

'No, we caught a *taxi* to 1952,' said Grandad sarcastically.

'This is amazing!' Frankie yelled, scrambling after him. 'I've never time-travelled before.'

'And I've never left a child in the middle of nowhere before, but today will be a day of firsts if you don't hurry,' huffed Grandad. 'We need to get to Hope Street again, and quickly.'

Then a thought struck Frankie. Not a good one. 'Grandad, how many times have you travelled back to 1952?'

'Does it matter?' the old man replied over his shoulder, with all the care and consideration of a professional wrestler.

'It matters a lot,' replied Frankie slowly. 'You see, Grandad, I've read a LOT of time-travel books and watched a LOT of time-travel movies … and if there's one thing I know, it's that if you keep going to the same point in time, you start to wear out the time path.'

Grandad stopped and stared at Frankie. 'Meaning?'

'Meaning things go wrong,' said Frankie, gesturing to the paddock around them. 'We end up in the middle of nowhere, instead of in the middle of **SOMEWHERE** …'

'You don't know what you're talking about,' Grandad snorted as he stomped off at top speed.

Frankie hurried after him. He didn't fancy being stuck out here – wherever *here* was – by himself.

You wouldn't expect there to be a train station in the middle of nowhere – or perhaps that's the perfect place for a train station – but either way, in the middle of the rolling green hills, there was one. It was only five minutes' walk from where Frankie and his grandad had landed.

It was a pretty basic set-up: just some tracks, which all good train stations should have, and a kiosk that was closed. All the same, Grandad seemed very relieved when they arrived.

'I think we just made it,' he said, puffing and red in the face from the brisk hike. Sure enough, trundling up to the platform was an old-school steam locomotive, like something out of *Thomas the Tank Engine*. Hissing and whistling, it lurched up to the platform before creaking to a stop.

Grandad sniffed. 'Well, that's one thing that's gone right today.'

Frankie followed him onto the train and into

a nearly empty carriage. Grandad went straight for a seat and slid along to the window side. Frankie rolled his eyes. Typical selfish Grandad. Everyone knew grandkids were supposed to get the window seat. Frankie slid into the next row and flopped his arms over the seat, so that he could look at Grandad.

But as the train started chugging along again, the old man's mind was clearly somewhere else. He was frowning deeply, and gripped the ruby suitcase so tightly that his knuckles were nearly white.

Frankie decided it was time for some answers. 'You have to tell me what's happening, Grandad. *Please*. Where the hell are we?'

(He wasn't really enjoying saying 'hell' anymore. Turns out swearing becomes less fun than you'd think when your parents have been turned into a fish-n-chip shop.)

Alfie Fish looked at his grandson. 'Francis, this is where I used to live.'

'You lived on a crappy old train in the middle of nowhere?' asked Frankie, bewildered.

'No, you fool,' Grandad snapped. 'This is Scotland.'

CHAPTER 8

THE SONIC SUITCASE

Frankie sat there, stunned, like he'd just found out that, um ... he had travelled back in time to Scotland in 1952.

He'd never been to Scotland. He'd never been to 1952 either.

'So ... why have we come here, exactly?' he managed to say, pulling himself together.

His grandad was silent for a long time, looking out the window at the fields flashing by.

'I sometimes feel like I'm losing my mind, lad,' he admitted. 'I forget things all the time.'

'Like that time you rang our house because you couldn't find your pants?' offered Frankie, stifling a smirk.

Another time, Grandad famously had forgotten to put his jocks on when he went down to the shops. Apparently it was only when he got to the frozen food aisle that he realised something wasn't right.

Grandad coughed. 'I don't remember that. Sometimes I forget little things, and sometimes big things.'

Frankie shrugged. 'We can all be a bit forgetful at times. Last week I forgot I had a Maths test.' This wasn't strictly true – Frankie just hated studying for Maths tests. But it seemed like Grandad needed some backup.

'Well, one day I woke up and I couldn't remember Nanna's name, and the doctor said it would probably get worse,' Grandad said, trembling a little. 'I thought if I went back in time, I could get my hand back and maybe my mind, too.'

Frankie had so many questions that he hardly knew where to start. 'So you decided to build a time-machine?'

'Well, actually – it's been my labour of love for sixty-five years. I once saw a magician make his assistant disappear, and I thought if he could do *that*, then maybe I could disappear back to *before* the accident.'

'And you built it in a suitcase because ...?'

'Makes it easy to carry!' Grandad smiled briefly.

'Also easy to steal,' said Frankie, putting this metaphysical puzzle together. 'That's why no-one was ever allowed in your shed.'

'Of course. If it got into the wrong grubby little hands, it could have been catastrophic.'

'But it didn't get into grubby little hands – it got into *your* old wrinkly hands, didn't it?'

Frankie retorted. 'Well, one wrinkly hand and a hook, anyway.'

'I admit I'm still figuring out some of this time-travel business,' Grandad said haughtily. 'There's a lot of mumbo jumbo about it that I still don't fully understand.'

'Well, the good news is that I *do*,' announced Frankie, proud that all those hours spent watching *Doctor Who* and *Back To The Future* were about to pay off.

Grandad looked Frankie right in the eye, like he was trying to decide if he could trust him.

Then, glancing around to make sure no-one was watching, Grandad opened the ruby suitcase a crack and removed a frayed notebook strapped inside the lid. He tapped it and looked at Frankie meaningfully. 'Do you know what's in this rule book?'

'Um – rules?' Frankie said uncertainly.

'Exactly. *Rules*.'

'How many are there?' asked Frankie, eyeing the bulging notebook.

'Look for yourself.' Grandad handed it to Frankie and then added crankily, 'But don't leave any boogers on it. Kids always leave boogers on everything.'

'Okaaaay,' said Frankie, deciding this wasn't the time to get into a generational argument about boogers. He opened the notebook and flicked through. There were pages and pages of complex mathematical sums and diagrams, but on the very last page was a neat list.

Some points were written in blue pen, some black pen, a couple in grey pencil – all in the same delicate cursive handwriting. Frankie began to read:

Important, must-follow rules and instructions for travelling with the Time Computer

'Time Computer?' Frankie asked, wrinkling his nose. 'You call it a **Time Computer?**'

'What's wrong with that? It's a computer and a time machine,' Grandad shot back. 'It describes it perfectly.'

'You didn't name the "orange" too, did you?' Frankie said cheekily. 'Nah, let's call it ... the Sonic Suitcase.'

'But it doesn't run on soundwaves, lad!' said Grandad. 'And it's almost completely silent.'

Frankie groaned. Had the old man never even heard of *Doctor Who?* 'Doesn't matter. It's a cool name.'

'Whatever. Ye can call it Gary for all I care.' Grandad's Scottish accent seemed to be getting thicker by the minute.

Frankie smiled and read a page with the first instruction.

1. TO SELECT YOUR DESTINATION:
Enter co-ordinates and set protective force field. To depart, type ‹HAPPYTRAVELS›.

'Wait, what force field?' Frankie asked.

'Am I going to have to explain every single thing to you?' snapped Grandad.

'Trust me, old man, I'll be the one explaining things to you soon enough,' Frankie said confidently.

Grandad sighed. 'The protective force field surrounds the shed and temporarily protects anything or anyone from the effects of changed historical events. It's so that we always have a place to return to safely.'

Something dawned on Frankie. 'Is that why I'm still here, even though ...?' He couldn't bring himself to say: *even though Nanna Fish and my parents don't exist anymore.* 'Is that why I haven't become Max's Fish-n-Chip shop? Because I was caught inside the force field when you went back the first time?'

'I guess so,' Grandad grunted.

'But why wouldn't you tell Nanna to get inside the force field to protect her?'

'I forgot, OK?' Grandad yelled defensively. 'That's enough questions for one day –'

But Frankie had begun piecing all the fragments of Grandad's story together. And there was one missing. 'Grandad ... how *did* you get your hand back exactly?'

The old man closed his eyes and swallowed hard. 'Here's the thing, boy,' he said. 'The Big Race of 1952 was the point where everything went wrong for me. Where on the final corner, I drove me beloved number 42 motorcar into the wall in a horrific crash, which spared me life but cost me my hand. So I went back and made sure I won. I beat me rival and arch-nemesis Clancy Fairplay once and for all. And I saved me hand.'

Frankie was confused. 'But why did that make Nanna disappear?'

Grandad shifted uncomfortably in his seat. 'Do ye not know how I met yer nanna?'

Frankie shrugged. 'It was in a hospital or something, wasn't it?' The details of the romance between his grandparents had never held much interest for him.

Grandad nodded. 'Aye, that's right. I was in hospital after I lost me hand, and Nurse Hopley cared for me.'

'Nurse Hopley?' Frankie replied, confused at this new name. 'Who the hell is Nurse Hopley?'

'Watch your mouth,' said Alfie. 'That's my wife you're talking about.'

'Of course! She's Nanna Fish!' Frankie exclaimed, smacking his forehead. 'So if you don't lose your hand, you don't meet Nurse Hopley, then Dad isn't born and if Dad isn't born ... I won't be born either.'

Frankie went very still for a moment, as all this sunk in. Clearly, his grandad had made a rookie time-traveller's mistake. One with *terrible* consequences. And suddenly Frankie was angry. **REALLY** angry.

'Grandad – you broke the number one rule of time travel,' Frankie hissed furiously. 'You don't fix things from the past. Mistakes and accidents have to remain mistakes and accidents, otherwise they become *bigger* mistakes and bigger accidents.'

Frankie gulped. He couldn't believe his grandad hadn't known that!

Grandad's shoulders slumped. 'I'm sorry, boy,' he muttered.

But Frankie barely heard him. Something the old man had said was nagging him. *The protective force field surrounds the shed and ...*

'... *Temporarily* protects anything or anyone,' Frankie echoed. 'Grandad? Any idea how long the force field lasts?'

'None at all,' Grandad confessed.

So I'm probably on borrowed time, thought Frankie grimly. Then he sat up straight. Did this have anything to do with Grandad's comments about his face?

Frankie peered into the window of the train, trying to catch a glimpse of his reflection.

It was difficult to make out much, but his eyes looked basically the same. Perhaps his cheeks were a little puffier than normal, but that could have been a side effect of time travel.

When he turned back, Grandad was looking into the Sonic Suitcase with a worried expression.

'What's wrong?' asked Frankie, feeling queasy.

'We need to move quickly,' Grandad said. 'The battery is already down to seventy-two per cent, and we need at least seventeen per cent to get us all the way home to 2017.'

Frankie raised an eyebrow. 'You didn't bring the charger with you?'

'Well,' Grandad muttered, 'it doesn't have a charger as such. It only charges at the bench.'

'The *bench?*' Frankie shot back, incredulous.

'The charging bench in the shed,' said Grandad, as if it were obvious.

'That's crazy,' said Frankie. 'Why wouldn't you just have a charger and a power point?'

'And what?' Grandad replied. 'Plug it into a power point in Ancient Greece? Find an adaptor in the Garden of Eden?'

'I guess not ...' Frankie said reluctantly. 'OK, fine, so we need to keep an eye on the battery.' Then he shivered. 'You know, this isn't just about us, Grandad,' he said, his voice rising above the rattling of the train. 'This affects the whole Fish family. Nanna, Dad, Mum, Lou ...'

'Aye, yer right,' said Alfie, biting his lip. He looked a lot older and far less confident than Frankie had ever seen him before. 'But listen, I have a plan. I can just *not win* that race, lose my hand and make everything right.'

Frankie sat back in his seat, the full magnitude of the situation horribly clear to him. His family had vanished, and he was in danger of disappearing at any moment, too. And his grandad's plan to fix things was definitely a long shot.

It was enough to reduce anyone to tears, and sure enough, a lump began forming in the back of Frankie's throat.

But as the train's horn bellowed out into the Scottish hills, something shifted inside him. A feeling that maybe he could be ... *responsible*, for a change. Save the day, even.

Frankie swallowed down the lump and slapped his hands on his knees. 'OK, Grandad,' he said firmly. 'Let's do this. Let's save the Fish family.'

Grandad looked at him strangely, with something almost like ... respect. 'Right you are, Francis.'

'Frankie,' said his grandson. 'My friends call me Frankie.'

CHAPTER 9

THE OTHER GRANDAD (IS NO BETTER THAN THIS GRANDAD)

The train soon arrived at a much bigger, busier station than the one where Frankie and Alfie had boarded. There was more hustle and a lot more bustle. People were getting on trains and people were getting off trains. Some in a rush, others in a daydream.

Frankie may have thought he was in a daydream, but he was *definitely* in a rush.

Alfie tightly gripped the ruby Sonic Suitcase with one hand, and kept the other on Frankie's forearm as they weaved through the crowd. As they dashed along, a thought occurred to Frankie.

'How did you win the race anyway, Grandad? It wasn't *you* in the car, was it?' he asked, trying to work out this mental jigsaw puzzle. 'I mean, the *you* I'm talking to now?'

'No no, Frankie – it was the younger me driving,' Grandad said.

'Then how did you change the outcome of the race?'

Grandad looked a bit sheepish. 'I just knocked on my door and when I answered, I gave myself some advice.'

'You spoke to ... you?!'

'Yep,' said the old man, fighting a naughty grin that Drew Bird would be proud of. 'I'd forgotten that I was such a handsome young devil.'

'What did you tell ... yourself?'

'I simply told *me* to avoid the oil spill on the final corner. So now all I have to do to put things right is to stop me from knocking on that door!' Alfie looked at his watch. 'Which the Other Grandad is going to do in approximately four minutes. So we'd better hurry.'

They dodged the daydreamers and exited Glasgow Central station, with Grandad setting a cracking pace.

'So how many of you are there right now?' Frankie asked while running, which is a rather tricky thing to do. It's for this very reason that schools don't teach Algebra and Cross Country at the same time.

Grandad thought for a moment. 'At this point, there are three. Me, the Other Grandad, and the Young Alfie.'

Three grandads! One was bad enough, Frankie thought to himself as he sprinted along.

As they ran, Frankie caught his first glimpses of Glasgow in 1952. He had always imagined history being in black and white, or brown and yellow tint – but amazingly, the world was in full colour. Some of the buildings still had damage from the war that Frankie had studied in History. The whole place looked run-down and dirty. Frankie even saw a couple of rats fighting over a scrap of food in the gutter.

The skies were grey and gloomy, but streets were still filled with people: couples strolling arm-in-arm, families out for the day. There were children on their own, playing in puddles and chasing each other in and out of alleyways, without a parent in sight. Boys poked each other with sticks and girls skipped rope, chanting rhymes. Frankie shook his head, feeling sorry for them. They'd never get to play Minecraft or own a Game Boy. If only they knew what they were missing out on.

'That's odd,' Grandad muttered as they ran. 'Could've sworn it was sunnier last time.'

'Huh?' said Frankie.

'Never mind,' Grandad huffed as he skidded around a corner. 'We're here.'

They were standing on Hope Street: the very street where Alfie Fish had grown up and, in this moment in time, still *did* live with his parents and younger brother Roddy.

Frankie had never seen anything like it. The houses were all squished up right next to each other, making one giant building that ran down the length of the street. Grandad made a beeline straight to number 42 at the end of the block. From behind him, Frankie saw their target: the Other Grandad, with the Other Sonic Suitcase swinging off his hook, about to knock on young Alfie's door.

Frankie could have fainted right there and then. Other Grandad was an **EXACT REPLICA** of Grandad, and as unsurprising as that was in theory, in reality it freaked Frankie out a little.

'Alfie!' yelled Grandad, at the top of his lungs.

'Don't do it!'

Frankie joined the chorus: 'Other Freaky Grandad, you're about to make a big mistake!'

Other Grandad's face was perplexed as he saw himself running towards him with his annoying grandson in tow. He had a look on his face like he'd just been busted stealing Nanna Fish's sweets from her special hiding spot in the pantry. His knuckles hung in mid-air, just inches away from the Fish family door.

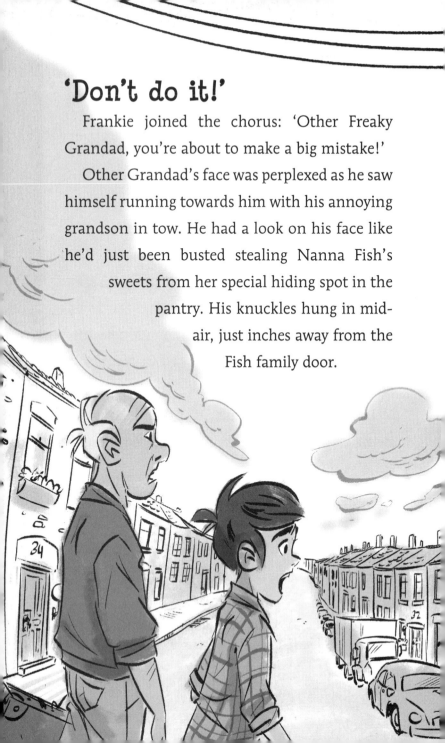

'What are you *doing*?' Other Grandad hissed. 'And what in blazes is *the boy* doing here? This is none of his business. And he'll probably leave boogers everywhere!'

'This **IS** my business,' Frankie hissed back.

'I've got the boogers under control, don't you worry,' said Grandad, closing in. 'Just get away from the door. You can't go through with this – the effects will be catastrophic!'

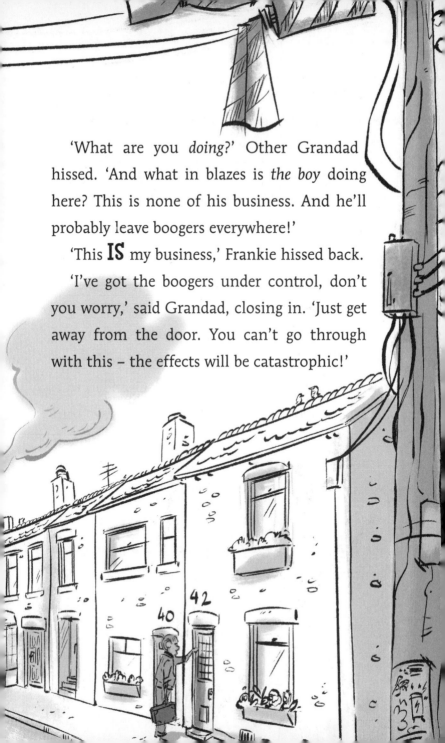

Grandad and Frankie stopped a few metres away, like police do in a hostage situation. Other Grandad looked like he was about to withdraw the clenched fist that lingered at the front door of the Fish family house. But then, as Other Grandad glanced down at his twin holding his Sonic Suitcase in his newly returned *right* hand, his face changed. His left and only fist tightened.

ᴋɴᴏᴄᴋ **KNOCK!**

'**NO!**' shouted Grandad. In one swift movement, he tossed his Sonic Suitcase to Frankie and lunged forward, wrapping Other Grandad in a rugby tackle. Then he hustled him away from the door and around the corner to a hidden pebbled alleyway.

'What are you doing?' complained Other Grandad, struggling against his attackers.

'Stopping you from making a big mistake, you old fool,' Grandad grunted. 'You changed the course of history and now everyone's gone – Mavis, Ron – *everyone*.'

'Also me,' Frankie added. 'Probably.'

'But you got your hand back!' Other Grandad said.

'It wasn't worth it,' Grandad replied firmly. 'Trust me. We need to send you back. Having three of me in the same time dimension could be disastrous. We should never have broken the rules. Frankie, get Other Grandad's Suitcase. We're sending him back and then we're going home too.'

'Right!' said Frankie, and spun around to grab the ruby suitcase. Except that it wasn't in the alley. 'Uh-oh ...'

The Other Sonic Suitcase was still in front of the house, where Other Grandad had dropped it.

In perfect sync, the two grandads said the exact same swear word. And it wasn't 'hell' or 'damn'.

CHAPTER 10

FISHY BUSINESS

The three Fish men collectively gulped and poked their heads around the corner like a set of terrible traffic lights – just in time to see the front door of the Fish family house opening. All three retreated faster than a rabbit after drinking too much red cordial.

The two Grandads and Frankie stood as still and silently as possible, listening carefully.

Somebody stepped outside and there was a scraping noise that sounded suspiciously like a suitcase being picked up off the ground. Then a cat's meow pierced the cold Glasgow air.

'Aw, that's Mr Wallace, our cat,' whispered Grandad. 'He was a cranky little thing – hated strangers and always used to steal our black pudding.'

'What's black pudding?' Frankie whispered.

'A sausage made from blood.'

Frankie gagged. Why would any person or cat eat, let alone *steal*, such a thing? **Yuck!**

The next moment, Mr Wallace came slinking around the corner. He stared up at the three Fish men frozen awkwardly against the wall, and then went right over to Other Grandad and started purring loudly.

'Mr Wallace, is that ye purring?' someone called from around the corner. It sounded like a young man. Maybe a young Alfie Fish? 'Have ye found a little friend?'

Mr Wallace meowed happily and loudly. Frankie closed his eyes, imagining the universe imploding at the exact moment the three Alfie Fishes laid eyes on each other.

'Mr Wallace?' the young man said again.

'Wash up for lunch, boys!' came a woman's voice from inside the house.

After another long, painful moment, they heard footsteps going back inside and the door closing with a bang.

The three Fish men breathed a sigh of relief. But the drama was just beginning. Once again, the three poked their heads around the corner and gave a collective gasp as they all saw the same thing ... *nothing*. The Other Sonic Suitcase was gone. Grandad groaned loudly.

'This is a disaster,' Frankie cried.

Other Grandad didn't seem to get it. 'It's OK. We still have this one,' he said, patting Grandad's Sonic Suitcase.

And that's when Frankie found some of his grandad's fireball ways. 'No, it's not OK at *all*,' he scolded. 'Haven't you seen *The Terminator*? Or *Back to the Future*? Or the third *Harry Potter* movie? Or – or – or even *Doctor Who*?!'

'Who?' replied Other Grandad, confused.

'**EXACTLY!**' replied Frankie. 'We **CANNOT** leave a time machine in the hands of unknowing people from the past. Anything could happen.' He sighed and shook his head. 'We need to send you home. The longer you stay, the worse the odds that trouble will find us.'

'But ... what if I don't want to go home?' asked Other Grandad.

'*What?*' came the dual voices of Grandad and Frankie.

'I like it here. My memory is clearer, and I feel more like myself,' Other Grandad said, staring off into the distance. 'The world feels safer than it does back home, too. And they'll probably let me drive as much as I want.' Then he leaned heavily against the wall.

There was a long silence. Frankie glanced at Grandad, and saw from his face that he felt the same way as his time-travel twin – at least a little bit.

Frankie leaned next to Other Grandad.

'I think I get what you mean, Other Grandad,' he said gently. 'I do. See, I made a mistake and now my school hates me, which is why I had to come stay with you for the school holidays even though I didn't want to – no offence.

'But even though I never want to go back to school, I know I have to because that's where my best friend Drew Bird is, and that's where my mum goes to pick me up, and where my annoying sister Lou is ...'

Frankie swallowed. He never thought it'd be possible, but he actually missed his dumb family. 'You need to go home, get me and come back, Other Grandad, so that we can stop you from ruining everything,' he said firmly. 'Nanna Fish *needs* you.'

His two grandads stared at him in astonishment. Frankie had surprised even *himself* with that speech, given that he wasn't much of a public speaker. The last time he'd done an oral presentation was in History class.

He was supposed to talk about Apollo 13, and he'd vomited from nerves before the shuttle left Houston. It wasn't a small vomit either – he blew chunks, *hard* chunks. Some carrot even landed on Mr Balconi's leather shoes (which was weird, because Frankie couldn't even remember the last time he'd eaten carrots).

Other Grandad looked up, his eyes welling with tears. 'But I'm scared,' he whispered.

'So am I,' Frankie whispered back. 'But it would be super weird if we *weren't* scared, considering the circumstances, right?' He smiled hopefully at Other Grandad.

Then something bizarre happened: Other Grandad smiled back.

'You're right,' said the old man. 'I'll go home with this suitcase, and you two can go recover mine.'

Then he took their Sonic Suitcase and squinted at the combination lock. 'Fifty-two per cent battery ... that'll be more than enough.

It loses its charge the longer you stay, but you only need –'

'Seventeen per cent to get back, I know,' Grandad interrupted Other Grandad. 'Just go already!'

And with the typing in of some co-ordinates, the use of the neighbour's backyard toilet without permission, and a muttered, '*Happy travels*,' the Other Grandad was gone.

CHAPTER 11

BUSTED

Now that Other Grandad was out of Scotland and out of their hair, Frankie and *this* Grandad could plot their next move. They needed to get the Other Sonic Suitcase back, and get it back fast.

'How about you distract them,' suggested Frankie, 'while I look for the case?'

'Good plan, boy,' said Grandad. 'Let's go!'

KNOCK KNOCK KNOCK!

The door was opened by a man younger than Grandad by about twenty-five years, but just as grumpy. 'What in the blazes do *ye* want?' he said in a thick Scottish brogue.

Grandad seemed to stand a little straighter. Frankie stared at the man's huge Christmas-ham fists, and realised this must be Grandad's *own* dad, Frankie's great-grandad Ernest Fish. Ernest was glaring expectantly and unwittingly at his own son, who was almost twice his age.

Weirdest. Day. Ever.

'Ahem,' Grandad said awkwardly, with a quiver in his voice that Frankie had never heard before. 'Um ... I'm sorry to bother you,' he said politely, 'but would you mind terribly if we used your lavatory? My grandson here, um ... er ... needs to poop.'

Frankie blushed. If anyone had bowel-control issues, it was the man who had farted at least fifty times since they arrived from the future.

'Is this true, lad?' asked the man sternly. 'Do ye need to **POOP?**'

Frankie briefly considered protesting his innocence, but reminded himself there was a bigger mission at stake. 'Yes, sir, I … I need to poop,' he replied, his cheeks hot.

'And by the whiff in my nostrils, it appears its arrival may be quite imminent!' pressed Grandad.

'Oh, come on,' muttered Frankie. He was suddenly grateful that the kids at school were sixty-five years into the future and would never find out about this.

The rather frightening-looking man sighed. 'OK, OK,' he said. 'The lav is upstairs. But mind ye don't leave any boogers on the walls!'

Seriously, what is it about this family and boogers? Frankie thought.

'I'll wait out here,' replied Grandad, as Frankie entered the house.

'Don't be daft,' said Ernest briskly. 'Come on in from the cold.'

Grandad reluctantly stepped inside his childhood home as Frankie headed for the stairs.

There was a funny smell in the air, like something had died. 'What *is* that?' Frankie said, sniffing. 'It smells like –'

'We're having haggis for lunch,' Ernest said. 'Special day and all. With neeps and tatties on the side.'

Frankie gave him the side-eye. **NEEPS** and **TATTIES?** He had no idea what they were, but he was pretty sure that saying it at school would get you three detentions with Miss Merryweather.

Then Grandad gave Frankie a shove, and he remembered that he was supposed to be saving the day. When Ernest was looking the other way, he lunged for the stairs.

'Can I get ye some tea?' Ernest asked Grandad. Then he squinted and added, 'Ye look familiar, ye know. Did ye know my father, Brian … Brian Fish?'

'I don't think so,' said Grandad, squirming. 'We're from out of town, just here for a quick visit.' He sounded reluctant to speak at all.

Good on you, Grandad, Frankie thought as he got to the top of the stairs. *Don't say a word!*

Upstairs, Frankie found four rooms. The first was a toilet, which was possibly the least likely room for somebody to keep a stolen suitcase. As expected, nothing. Behind the next door was a bedroom. Nothing again.

Frankie crept into the third room, another bedroom. There he found not the suitcase, but a familiar-looking man snoring with his mouth wide open, as happy as a pig in suspiciously stinky mud. Frankie froze. It was a young Alfie Fish.

Frankie backed out quickly, puzzled. Grandad hadn't mentioned anything about his younger self being asleep when he came to give him advice. And if that hadn't been young Alfie opening the front door ... who was it?

Frankie tried to ignore his creeping sense of unease. At least young Alfie being asleep kept him and old Alfie apart this time.

The floorboards let out tiny creaks as Frankie sneaked across them, as quickly as he dared. He knew it was only a matter of time before someone came up to check on him – or before young Alfie woke up and caught him. The suitcase had to be here somewhere.

Glancing towards the end of the upstairs hallway, Frankie Fish felt a rush of delight. There, just visible through the crack in the doorway, was the Sonic Suitcase, sitting patiently against the wall. Frankie just had to grab it and then he and his grandad could go home.

He moved nimbly through the door and leapt for the –

'May I help ye?' came a voice from behind him.

Frankie cringed, and slowly turned around. **Busted.**

CHAPTER 12

UNCLE RODDY

Frankie saw a boy of about fifteen, sitting by the window, surrounded by butcher's paper and coloured pencils. It looked like they were in a study.

'Looking for something?' the boy asked knowingly.

Frankie realised that he'd been stupid not to check the room before barging in. He also

realised that this must be his great-uncle Roddy, whom Grandad hadn't spoken to in forty years.

'Hi,' said Frankie, trying to sound casual, and failing.

Roddy just looked at him, and then put his pencil down on a nearby sketch. It was a rough outline of what was obviously two old men fighting over a suitcase. Next to it was a more detailed drawing of a steam train, not unlike the one Frankie and Grandad had taken into Glasgow. The drawing was amazing. Every line was perfect, like the train might chug right off the page.

Roddy stood up slowly. 'Look here, kid,' he

said in a low voice. 'I know this suitcase belongs to ye and that weird old man downstairs, and I know he just had a fight with *another* old man who looks exactly like him, AND that both those old men look a lot like my father. I'm assuming it was *them* that Mr Wallace went right up to before, which he never does to strangers, the grumpy little git. Something *fishy* is going on here, so give me one good reason why I shouldn't scream out loud right now and have my father call the police?'

Frankie gulped, not sure what to do. And really, what were his options? The truth probably wouldn't go down well. And even if he could get over the thought of jumping through a glass window to escape, they were on the second floor. Which only left option three: lying. The words glided past his tongue and out of his mouth.

'My grandad's twin has a medical condition and the medicine he needs is in that suitcase.'

Roddy raised an eyebrow. 'What is the medical condition, exactly?' he asked curiously.

'Um,' said Frankie, flustered. He didn't know of any medical conditions. 'I forget what it's called, but the main symptoms are extreme gas, severe crankiness and delusions.'

Roddy's eyes narrowed. 'What kind of delusions?'

'Well ... sometimes he thinks he's been sent from the future, which is pretty super weird. Last night in his sleep he was saying he was King of the Planet Netflix and he needed to get back to save Queen Twitter by logging into Facebook on his iPod,' explained Frankie, who realised he was having way too much fun all of a sudden. 'Like I said, he is **SUPER WEIRD** without his medication.'

'What a strange man he must be,' Roddy mused.

The two boys stared at each other for a moment. Frankie felt a little bead of sweat dribble down his back.

'Fine,' Roddy muttered, and sat down again heavily. 'Just take it. Wouldn't make a difference if you were lying, anyway. My family wouldn't listen to me if I told them to call the police. There's only one thing they care about, and that's racing.'

Frankie allowed himself one small sigh of relief. He picked up the suitcase, looking around the room he did so. He was surprised to find that it was an almost exact replica of the Not-So-Forbidden Shed back in 2017, but with a lot less dust. The shelves were lined with trophies and photographs of young Alfie in cars, holding prizes and grinning like a loon. Framed newspaper articles declared **'FISH NEW FORCE IN MOTORSPORTS'** and **'FAIRPLAY MEETS NEW CHALLENGER'**.

Then he realised something else. All the photographs and all the newspaper clippings were of Grandad, and not a single one was of Great Uncle Roddy.

Roddy was ignoring Frankie now, and had returned to his drawing.

Frankie didn't need to be a fancy art expert to see that Roddy had talent. His drawings were phenomenal. There were drawings of wartime aircraft, and buildings, and even a small sketch of a racing car with a familiar man leaning casually against it.

Frankie wondered what that must have been like for Roddy. He sure knew what it was like to grow up in your brother's – or in Frankie's case, *sister's* – shadow. But this seemed bigger than that. It seemed sadder.

Before Frankie could even understand the emotion he was feeling, he heard the voice of Great-Grandma Iris screaming from downstairs.

'Roddy, ye put away those **SILLY DRAWINGS** and come downstairs **RIGHT NOW**. I didn't spend the morning stuffing **OFFAL** and **OATMEAL** into a sheep's **STOMACH** for it to go to waste! Just because ye don't want to come along and **SUPPORT YER BROTHER** this afternoon at the Big Race does not mean yer **EXCUSED** from **LUNCH** with yer **FAMILY!**' There was a pause, and then she added: 'And **WAKE YER BROTHER UP FROM HIS NAP** while yer at it!'

Frankie heard Roddy sigh as he started to pack up his papers and pencils. He thought of Saint Lou, and how his parents were always proud of her, and how it made him sad because he never seemed able to do things that made them proud of him, too.

Frankie felt another bunch of words glide over his tongue and into the world. 'Your dad was telling us downstairs that you're an *amazing* artist, you know,' he said. 'He told us you'd be world-famous one day. Just like your brother.'

Roddy didn't lift his head from his sketch. But Frankie saw a tinge of pink appear in his cheeks.

Frankie hoped he was doing the right thing. 'He sure seemed *equally* proud of you both,' he added. 'Anyway, I'd better go. See you around.'

Roddy nodded, a tiny smile on his face. 'See ye 'round.'

With that, Frankie bounded back down the stairs with the Sonic Suitcase, away from the study and his Great Uncle Roddy, whom he knew he'd probably never see again.

As he got to the bottom, he heard the radio crackling away in a nearby room.

'*Who do you fancy to take out the Big Race, William?*' an announcer was saying. '*Fairplay or Fish?*'

'Ooh, look, they're both excellent drivers, but I just can't go past that Clancy Fairplay. He's not as slippery as Fish, but he definitely has the superior skill –'

The radio was suddenly turned off. Frankie, now peering into the kitchen, saw Ernest shaking his head vigorously. 'Clancy Pompouspants, more like. They don't know **WHAT** they're talking about. I wouldn't trust them to iron my trousers! What do you say, erm – what's your name again, chap?' he said to his son from the future.

'Oh, there you are, boy,' Grandad said, dodging the question and leaping to his feet. 'Did you remember to wipe your bum?'

Frankie couldn't quite work out if Grandad was deliberately trying to embarrass him, or if he just didn't know at what age you can stop asking those types of questions. 'Yes, Grandad, I did everything I needed to do,' he replied through gritted teeth. 'We can go now.'

'Of course, of course,' Ernest said, ushering them to the door. 'That's one hell of a nice suitcase you have there. I don't remember seeing it when you arrived,' he added, a little suspiciously.

'Must have been out of view,' Grandad said, nudging Frankie. 'We don't travel anywhere without it, do we Frankie?'

Behind Ernest, Frankie saw young Alfie Fish wandering sleepily down the stairs. Tugging on his grandad's hand, he hissed, 'Let's go!'

'I must be getting old,' mused Ernest.

'Aye, it happens to all of us, Fa–' Grandad coughed. 'I mean, *chap*. Thanks again, best be off!'

And with that our two time travellers hurried away from the Fish household.

CHAPTER 13

A CHANGE OF WEATHER = A CHANGE OF DESTINY

Frankie and Grandad made their way quickly through a nearby park, Grandad looking as though he'd got an obese elephant off his chest.

'It's time to go back then, isn't it?' Grandad said, patting the Sonic Suitcase. 'We stopped Other Me from giving *Young* Me advice, so he'll lose the race like last time and then everything will go back to normal.'

But Frankie was staring up at the sky with dread. Heavy storm clouds were moving rapidly across the Glasgow sky. 'This is not good,' he said, as it began to spit.

'A bit of rain never hurt anyone,' replied a chirpy Grandad. 'It's good for the farmers.'

'Well, it's not good for the Fishes.'

'Why's that?' replied Grandad.

'You said that the last time you came here it was **SUNNY**, right?' Frankie asked. A freezing cold wind began to blow.

'Weather changes all the time,' Grandad said. 'It doesn't mean anything.' But he didn't sound so sure anymore.

Frankie shook his head. 'But it *does*. I've read about this – when different things happen in the same timeline, it means there's been some kind of simultaneity breakdown.'

Grandad looked over one shoulder, then the other. 'I'm sorry, did you think you were speaking with Albert Einstein or something?'

Frankie didn't smile. 'This is really bad, Grandad. You don't understand –'

'Frankie, you're getting worked up over nothing,' Grandad interrupted, as thunder rumbled in the distance. He gestured to the Sonic Suitcase, where the battery was sitting at forty-two per cent. 'We've done what we came to do. Now let's just get home before –'

'You don't *understand*,' Frankie said, raising his voice to compete with the gathering storm. 'We've meddled with time and now the future is muddled!'

Cue thunder claps as the two Fish men ran to take cover in a nearby rotunda.

'*Muddled?*' Grandad repeated. He had lost all his chirpiness now, like a canary with laryngitis.

'When you came back a **SECOND** time to the same place, you messed with the time path,' said Frankie tightly. '*That made today more unpredictable*. Think about it, Grandad. You landed the Sonic Suitcase in the wrong place without meaning to. The weather is **TOTALLY** different now than it was before –'

'And young Alfie was asleep this time, instead of answering the door,' finished Grandad slowly. 'You mean things are different this time just *because* we came back?'

Frankie nodded. 'And now that it's raining, anything could happen. They could cancel the Big Race entirely.'

Grandad went pale. 'How about we go back home and if it doesn't work, we can come back and fix it again?' he suggested desperately.

Frankie sat down on a bench in the rotunda, exhausted by his own explanation. 'That could make things even worse. The more we go back and forth to the same point in time, the more we destabilise the timeline and wear out our time path.' He shook his head. 'No. We need to stay for the Big Race. We need to make sure it turns out the way it's supposed to.'

Grandad clenched his fists. Frankie knew

this was NOT what he wanted to hear. The old man wanted to type those co-ordinates into that stupid computer and get them back to 2017. Frankie hoped he'd see that he was right.

As the silence stretched out, Frankie remembered his conversation with Roddy, and what he'd said at the end. He felt sick. He'd thought he was doing the right thing, but who knew how much damage he might have caused?

Finally, Grandad nodded sadly. 'We don't have a choice, aye.'

Frankie sagged, relieved. 'Nope, we really don't.' He crossed his fingers for luck, and then helped Grandad to his weary feet. 'The Big Race is just over an hour away, so we need to hurry across town. We just have to hope that the race plays out exactly as it did – the *first* time around.'

Mercifully, the rain stopped, though the skies were still dark and grey as Frankie and Grandad jogged briskly through the old streets of Glasgow.

Now, Frankie had the edge on his grandad about time travel, but the old man knew the streets of his hometown like the back of an ageing hand.

'I know a shortcut,' he told Frankie, leading him to a pair of rather intimidating rusty metal gates. Leaves danced in the breeze and the steel chain that held the gates together rattled loudly. Beyond them was what appeared to be an imposing school building.

'We can squeeze through here,' Grandad told his grandson with a cheeky grin. He held the gates apart as Frankie slipped through, and then followed after him.

Frankie wasn't exactly sure why, but once on the other side of the gates, Grandad suddenly had a spring in his tired old step.

Whistling, the old man strode through the school grounds, pointing things out to Frankie – his favourite monkey bars, and then the football pitch where he'd once dreamt of playing for Celtic and eventually Liverpool.

'This is great, Grandad,' said Frankie, 'but we need to get to the Big Race.'

But Grandad didn't seem to hear him. He pointed through a dusty classroom window and explained to Frankie that this was where he and his mate Lenny McGregor had once pranked their headmaster. 'Mr McGinley never saw it coming, the old fool,' he smirked.

Frankie was stunned. 'You did *pranks?*' he asked, forgetting about the Big Race for a moment. It was like hearing that Old Man Harris had once sung a Beyoncé song on *X-Factor*.

'Yeah, me and Lenny hooked up a dead rat on a fishing hook and lowered it onto McGinley's head as he was saying the morning prayer,' Grandad said, a conspiratorial glint in his eye.

'He was bald, so it looked for a few seconds like he had a bad wig. Everyone loved it! Well, not McGinley ... and probably not Jesus either.'

He chuckled happily, and dabbed his eyes with a handkerchief.

Frankie grinned, though he couldn't imagine himself getting so emotional about going back to school when he was 120 (although actually, Grandad was only eighty-five).

But maybe time does funny things to you,
Frankie thought. *Certainly time-travelling does.*
Then, with a jolt, Frankie suddenly remembered
why they were there.

He tugged urgently on Grandad's arm. 'The race starts in less than forty minutes, so –'

'Yeah, yeah, I know,' Grandad grunted as he led Frankie out of the school. 'Keep your hair on.'

'One of us has to,' said Frankie, but quietly, so that his nearly bald grandad didn't hear.

They kept walking at a good pace, down the street, past some old factories billowing smoke and up to a building marked **St Mary's Hospital**. 'Let's have a breather,' said Grandad, puffing loudly.

Frankie looked at his watch. The Big Race start time was rapidly approaching, and they needed to get to the speedway soon, but his grandad did look like he needed a short break. 'OK, one minute,' Frankie said, his jaw tight. Time, quite obviously, was **NOT** on their side.

Grandad looked at the hospital entrance and then down at Frankie, his eyes twinkling. 'I want you to meet, or at least see, the most beautiful woman in the world ...' Then he slipped quickly between the hospital's emergency-department doors.

'*Grandad –*' Frankie screeched, following him into St Mary's Hospital. 'We do **NOT** have time to look for your old-lady girlfriend!'

But he stopped short when his grandad pointed out a pretty, young nurse at the nursing station, her brown hair pinned up under a hat. As they watched, the nurse turned around to call for someone, and Frankie caught sight of some very familiar bright blue eyes.

'Is that ... *Nanna?*' Frankie gasped.

Grandad let out a little laugh. 'Technically she's still Nurse Mavis Hopley. She only becomes Nanna Fish when I marry her, and we have your father and then your father has you and your sister Lou.'

He took two steps forward, but his grandson clutched his jacket.

'Grandad!' Frankie hissed. 'No, you can't.

We can't, it's too risky! And we **REALLY** need to go.'

Grandad looked wistfully at Nurse Hopley. 'Just a quick hello?'

'Remember the rules?' grimaced Frankie. 'That quick hello could change everything.'

'I guess you're right,' Grandad said reluctantly.

With this reassuring declaration, Frankie let go of his grandad's jacket ... but as he did, the old man raised the back of his hand to his forehead and crumpled to the ground.

CHAPTER 14

TRICKY OLD FOOL

Frankie dropped to his knees and nursed his grandad's head. 'Grandad! Grandad!'

No response.

'Everybody move back,' came the eerily familiar voice of Nurse Hopley. The crowd reluctantly dispersed as Nurse Hopley knelt at Alfie Fish's side. 'What's his name?' she asked Frankie, who was rendered speechless.

Then suddenly Grandad's eyes popped open like a six-year-old's on Christmas morning. 'Alfred's my name,' he announced, 'and I am so sorry, but I appear to have fainted.'

Nurse Hopley helped Grandad to his feet, and as he rose he gave Frankie a wink. *What a tricky old fool*, Frankie thought to himself.

'Are you feeling OK?' Nurse Hopley asked Grandad with concern.

'I'm feeling *quite* wonderful. Say, has anyone ever told you how beautiful your eyes are?' Alfie murmured, as Frankie looked around for a sick bag.

'Oh, we are a sweet talker, aren't we?' Nurse Hopley laughed.

'Grandad, we really need to get going,' urged Frankie, looking at the clock on the wall.

'I suppose you're off to the Big Race then, like everyone else?' smiled Nurse Hopley. 'I'm working, but I'm going to listen to it on the radio. Depending on the outcome, I might have a date tonight with a dashing young driver.'

'Is that right?' chuckled Grandad, clearly assuming that she meant a date with his younger self.

Nurse Hopley flushed the colour of a tomato trapped in a lava lamp. 'I don't normally share personal information like that with strangers,' she said, 'but I feel like I know you somehow.' She stared at Grandad like she was trying to work out the answer to a question she didn't understand. 'Have we met before? You look so familiar.'

'N-no,' Grandad stammered, and then added, 'Although some people think I look like a young Mick Jagger.' (No they don't.)

'Mick *who?*' asked Nurse Hopley.

'Never mind him,' said Grandad quickly. 'Who is the lucky driver?'

Nurse Hopley flushed even deeper. 'Clancy Fairplay,' she blurted. 'He was a patient here once, had a nasty bout of gout, and he's been pestering me ever since for a date. I finally said I'd have dinner with him if he wins the Big Race today. He's a bit full of himself, but a promise is a promise.'

Grandad groaned loudly.

Nurse Hopley looked worried. 'Sir, you've gone a little pale,' she said. 'Are you going to faint again?'

Grandad shook his head.

'He's fine,' said Frankie hastily, pulling his grandad towards the exit. 'Sorry, we've got to get going. Thanks, bye!'

Nurse Hopley gave them a confused wave and, with a strange look, turned back to her station.

'A date with *Clancy Fairplay*?' Grandad moaned as they left the building. 'Mavis never mentioned anything about that before. Not in over fifty years of marriage.'

Frankie had gone cold. Was this yet *another* example of time breaking down?

Thunder clapped above them.

Frankie felt a sudden urge to look in the mirror. 'Grandad, how's my face?' he asked worriedly.

Grandad glanced at him. 'It's weird, like normal,' he snapped. 'But we've got bigger fish to fry, Frankie. If Clancy wins the race, I could *still* lose Mavis. And if I win the race, I lose ...'

'Everybody,' finished Frankie. 'We **ALL** lose.'

CHAPTER 15

WORST
ICE-CREAM EVER

The track was only a few hundred metres from the hospital, and the road was full of racing fans making their way to the Big Race. Men walked with children on their shoulders and kids waved colourful homemade flags. There were festive chants, feverish cheering and fitful clapping.

But the mood of the two Fish men was entirely

different. The excitement of their whirlwind tour had been replaced with a much heavier feeling. Things were *not* looking good for the future of the Fish family.

As they neared the entrance to the track, Grandad suddenly stopped and bent down. For a minute Frankie thought he had 'fainted' again, but he came up holding a coin in his right hand.

'About time we had some good luck,' said Grandad. There was a little spark in his eyes as if he had just had an idea. 'Do you like ice-cream, Frankie?'

'Of course. I'm a kid,' replied Frankie, thinking that it was like asking an old person if they enjoyed sleeping in front of the TV or farting during family dinners.

'Go over there and buy yourself one,' Grandad said, pointing to nearby shop. 'Get topping if you want it, too.'

Frankie couldn't believe it. He was *never* allowed to get topping. He bit his lip, torn – they only had twenty minutes until the race started, but then again ... if he was **VERY** quick, and surely he'd more than earned it today ...

'Do you want one too?'

'No thanks, I'm watching my figure,' replied Grandad. 'Here, give me the suitcase. I'll hold it while you get your ice-cream. I'll wait right here.'

'OK, I'll be super quick,' Frankie said, dashing off. Just as he was about to enter the ice-cream parlour, Grandad called out to him. 'Frankie!'

Frankie turned around.

'You're not such a bad kid after all,' Grandad said. 'I'm very happy to be sharing this adventure with you.'

Frankie felt a grin spread across his face. 'Thanks, Grandad. You're not so bad yourself.' Then he disappeared into the ice-cream parlour to make the painful and urgent decision between chocolate and strawberry.

The shop was empty, except for a young man in

a pointy white hat behind the counter, listening to the radio. Two commentators were excitedly discussing the Big Race. Frankie pressed up against the glass, trying to decide which way to go.

Too. Hard. To. Choose.

'Excuse me, sir,' Frankie asked the attendant, flashing his money. 'How much ice-cream does this get me?'

The man squinted at the coin. 'Two cones, two scoops each, plus topping.'

Frankie stared at him. 'No way!'

In 2017, a single coin would barely pay for the cone itself. Frankie had the extraordinary idea of having one scoop of chocolate and one scoop of strawberry with caramel sauce.

As the Pointy-Hat Man started scooping ice-cream, a pompous voice boomed from the radio.

'*The racing of the race is merely a formality,*' the voice said. '*We all know who the best driver in all of Scotland is … It's* **ME**, *Clancy Fairplay. And let me tell you something else, not only will I win* the Big Race, but I'll also win the heart and hand of the most beautiful woman in Glasgow, Miss Mavis Hopley!' he declared, like Nanna Fish was a prize to collect.

'Clancy Fairplay? That man is such a scoundrel that even his name lies,' scoffed Pointy-Hat Man. 'That germ doesn't have a fair bone in his body. If he even **THINKS** of coming into **THIS** shop again, he'll have another thing coming.'

'Why?' asked Frankie.

'I had to toss him out of here a week ago,' the man snorted. 'He slapped a child just because he asked him for an autograph.'

'That's terrible!' gasped Frankie. He thought that if he ever saw Clancy Not-so-Fairplay in person, he'd kick him right where the sun don't shine (though in Scotland, that could be anywhere).

Clancy's voice kept blathering on as Pointy-Hat Man piled the strawberry scoop on top of the chocolate. *'Alfie Fish may be fast, but he lacks the control and discipline it takes to be a great driver. He makes emotional decisions. If he were on my team, I'm not sure I would trust him to do what he says he'll do.'*

As Pointy-Hat Man handed Frankie the towering cone of ice-cream in exchange for the coin, Frankie's mind began racing. His smile, which a minute ago had been as wide as a pair of elephant's speedos, was now as narrow as sparrow's bowtie. Clancy Fairplay's words replayed in his head: *'I'm not sure I would trust him to do what he says he'll do.'*

Frankie hurriedly left the ice-cream parlour, his cone trembling. Grandad had said he'd wait for him on the other side of the street.

But Grandad was gone.

A lady in a fur coat approached, carrying a small, shaggy dog. It was difficult to make out where the dog ended and the coat began.

'Are you Frankie? Frankie Fish?' she asked

in a thick Scottish accent. If she wasn't saying Frankie's own name, he wasn't sure he would have understood her.

'Yes,' he replied meekly as a trickle of chocolate ice-cream ran down his thumb.

'Your grandad asked me to tell you he had to go and make things right,' she explained. 'He said he'll see you when he's done.'

Frankie had a bad feeling in the pit of his stomach. He hardly noticed as the strawberry

scoop slipped off his cone onto the wet cobblestones. Then the chocolate one slid off after it, like the world's sweetest avalanche.

'Oh, you dropped your ice cream ...' said the Furry Lady, as her dog went crazy and struggled to the ground. 'Ruffles *loves* ice-cream.'

Ruffles did love ice-cream. His fat little tongue lashed all over Frankie's favourite sneakers, but Frankie was too preoccupied to notice.

Surely this is a mistake, Frankie thought as he swung his head from left to right to try and spot his grandad.

'Which way did he go?' Frankie asked the Furry Lady, who was taking great delight in Ruffles' ice-cream haul.

'That way, dear,' she said, pointing down the road in the direction of the Big Race. 'Are you feeling OK? Your face looks a little ... funny.'

Frankie pressed his fingers into his face as he looked into the butcher's window at his reflection. Somehow his eyes looked narrower and his cheeks were fatter.

This. Is. Not. Good!

'I'm fine,' muttered Frankie, as he hurried away. But he wasn't fine. Frankie's head was full of thoughts, none of them very funny at all.

He knew that Grandad was upset that Nanna was possibly going on a date with his arch nemesis, the arrogant, dim-witted Clancy Bumface.

He also knew that Grandad, for all his flaws, was crazy about Nanna Fish, and would do everything in his power to stop that from happening.

Which could only mean one thing: Grandad was on his way to talk to Young Alfie Fish. He was either going to make the same mistake all over again – or worse yet, he might confess **EVERYTHING** about their time-travelling, in which case the authorities would lock him up forever and throw away the key, because he would sound INSANE.

Either way, it meant that Frankie – and his family – would disappear forever.

Worst. Ice-Cream. Ever.

CHAPTER 16

THE SAME MISTAKE,
THE SAME MISTAKE

Frankie Fish ran as fast as he could through the Glaswegian streets, following the swarms of race fans in their raincoats on their way to the speedway. What those excited motorsport fans didn't know, and what the boy panting as he ducked and weaved around them knew only too well, was that there was a lot more at stake today than the reputation of a couple of racecar drivers.

Without **ONE BIT OF INTERFERENCE WHATSOEVER**, Young Alfie simply *had* to skid his car through the oil spill and crash into the wall in order to allow Clancy Fairplay to win. The Big Race was no longer just a race. Frankie's life – and the lives of the entire Fish family – *depended* on Grandad crashing.

Frankie **HAD** to find Grandad before he said anything to change that outcome.

Frankie darted around the waists and past the legs of excited race-goers, all the time looking out for the old man. 'Grandad!! Grandad Fish!!!' he screamed.

The closer he got to Pit Lane, the denser the crowd became – it seemed everyone wanted to catch a glimpse of the fast cars and the brave men who drove them. Then Frankie spotted a child tugging on Clancy Fairplay's sleeve for an autograph, only for the driver to swat him away like a fly.

What a jerk, Frankie said to himself.

The crowd was building by the second. Frankie couldn't squeeze any closer, so he headed for the nearby grandstand. He knew that if he got up a little higher, he'd have a bird's eye view and a better chance of spotting Grandad. And sure enough, halfway up the stairs he spotted him – but the news wasn't good.

Grandad was standing in Pit Lane, where all the cars and their drivers were lined up, talking to Young Alfie Fish.

Frankie filled his lungs full of air and screamed, **'GRANDDAAAAAAADDD!!!!'** as he waved both arms in the air like somebody drowning at sea.

Maybe Grandad couldn't hear his grandson bellowing or maybe he conveniently chose to ignore him. Either way, he didn't move a muscle.

Frankie felt his heartbeat quickening. There was a lump in his throat the size of a pineapple. This had disaster written all over it.

He had no way of knowing whether Grandad Alfie was instructing Young Alfie to avoid the oil spill so that he could marry Nanna, or telling him about their time-travel mess-ups – either way Frankie Fish was basically dead, and that would not be good at all for Frankie OR the future of this book series.

'**Noooooooooooooooo!!!!!**' screamed Frankie as he leapt down the grandstand steps, knocking over the man selling soda and sweets.

Frankie darted his way through the crowd, puffing and panting all over again. It got harder and harder to squeeze past the people, until out of sheer desperation he dived to the ground and began crawling through the legs of the buzzing fans.

'Grandad!' Frankie cried out.

Both Alfies turned to see their grandson on his knees.

'You need to **STOP MEDDLING!**' Frankie

yelled, before turning his attention to Young Alfie Fish, who looked very dashing in his racing uniform, helmet tucked under his arm. 'Don't believe a single word he says,' Frankie told him furiously. His eyes felt rather hot all of a sudden. 'He's just a crazy old man, selfish and rude and mean and deluded!'

Young Alfie Fish looked extremely confused. 'He was just asking for an autograph for his grandson, Frankie. Who are you?'

Frankie looked up as sheepishly as a sheep dressed in sheep's clothing. 'Oh. Um, I'm Frankie.' Frankie looked at Grandad, who looked like the cat that used ice-cream to trick his grandson. 'Are you sure that's all he said?'

'Yep,' said Alfie, shooting him a devilishly handsome grin, before adding, 'He gave me some good advice, too.'

Gulp.

'What was the advice?' Frankie asked, wincing.

'To drive as fast as he possibly can,' Grandad said quietly. 'Full throttle, like this is his last race. Don't leave anything in the tank.'

'I never do, old chap,' Young Alfie said, clapping Grandad on the back. 'I never do.' Then he handed his autograph to Frankie.

Frankie stared at it, feeling his tummy slowly unclench. 'Huh,' he said. Then he looked up and said, 'Can I post this on Facebook when we get home?'

'Uh, you can post it to whoever you like,' Young Alfie replied, a little confused. 'Anyway, nice to meet you, chaps.'

As his young grandfather turned to go, Frankie suddenly found an image of Roddy flashing through his mind. Before he had a chance to reconsider, he blurted out, 'You know, your brother really looks up to you.'

Young Alfie – and Grandad – stared at him in surprise. 'You know Roddy?' said Young Alfie.

'Er, we've met,' said Frankie. He *knew* he

should stop, but the words just kept coming. 'You know, you should pay him some attention. Because one day he might vanish for good and then you'll realise what you've lost. I mean, I always found my sister super annoying, but now she's gone ...' He finally managed to stop, feeling strangely choked up.

Young Alfie looked at him weirdly, then nodded and offered his hand to Frankie. Frankie took it, remembering to make it a firm grasp like his dad had taught him. Then Young Alfie reached out to Grandad, who stared at the perfect right hand for a second before taking it in his own.

Three generations of Fishes, meeting in a fashion that no three generations had ever met before, and will probably never meet again. Frankie silently instructed his brain to remember this moment forever.

'Are you going to watch the race?' Young Alfie asked.

Frankie understood that this might be a painful event for Grandad to watch, so he shook his head. 'We'll probably just stream it later,' he said hopefully.

'Yes,' interrupted Grandad, as politely as he'd ever interrupted anyone before. 'Yes, we're going to stay here and watch the whole race. Make sure we get the result we need.'

'Great,' said Young Alfie. 'But, er, can you let go of my hand now?'

CHAPTER 17

THE BIG RACE

Grandad and Frankie managed to find two seats looking over the final corner – the infamous corner where Alfie Fish lost control of his beloved machine before it careered into the wall. Frankie was so nervous that he felt like he'd swallowed a jar full of bees.

As the smell of engines and gasoline danced around Frankie Fish's nose, the racetrack's loudspeaker buzzed and crackled to life.

'*Untimely and unexpected grey skies overhead won't dull the thousands of fans who've flocked to the track today to see the much anticipated Big Race. I haven't been this excited since my wife allowed me to eat black pudding in my undies on my birthday, but that is probably too much information for now. Many believe the Big Race is down to just two competitors, Clancy Fairplay and Alfie Fish ...*'

A roar rose from the crowd when the commentator mentioned Alfie Fish's name. Little did anyone know there were two Alfie Fishes at the track that day. Young Alfie in racecar number 42, and Grandad Alfie, who was watching with his grandson in the *grand*stand – and what a *grand* occasion it was.

It's super weird to hear the crowd cheering for Grandad, thought Frankie. Almost like hearing the students at St Monica's cheering and whooping for Principal Dawson at assembly. The crowd had the exact opposite reaction to

Clancy Fairplay's name being announced. There was moderate applause sprinkled with boos and jeers, and some rude Scottish words that can't be printed in a nice book like this.

The commentator's voice became more excited.

'Mark this date down in history lads and lassies, today will be remembered as the birth of a famous sporting rivalry. In years to come when people talk about motorsport they won't be able to avoid talking about Fairplay versus Fish in the Big Race. There is **NO** *doubt about it, today will be a* **CLASSIC!**'

Grandad's knee was shaking like a leaf stuck to a milkshake machine in an earthquake. Frankie tried to stop it by covering it with his own hand, but unfortunately Frankie's hand was shaking too so it was no help at all.

Frankie glanced upwards at the sky. The rain seemed to be holding off, but for how much longer?

In his short life, Frankie had been nervous many times. Like when they dissected a frog in a Science exam. Or when he'd performed as a Wise Man in a nativity play. And there was the time he'd had to tell his dad about the D- he received for his Biology project about electric eels (which Ron Fish had helped with, which made it worse). But Frankie had **NEVER** been *this* nervous.

His nerves felt like they were full of electricity. All the hairs on his body stood at right angles. It was like every single part of his body knew that if this race didn't end with Grandad crashing and *losing*, then Frankie might just vanish into thin air.

As the cars drove up to the start line, Frankie looked up at Grandad with a sense of pride. All these people were here to see his grandad, to cheer him on! But Grandad didn't seem to notice the cheers. He just sat there with his eyes closed, gripping the ruby suitcase tightly.

'Would you like to leave, Grandad?' asked Frankie.

'No, kiddo. I'm OK, but thanks for asking,' replied Alfie.

And with that, the race began. **CRACK!**

The crowd roared as Alfie and Clancy immediately began vying for the lead. It was beyond loud at the track, louder than a fireworks display in a barnyard. And with every lap, every daring move, the noise of the cars and of the crowd seemed to intensify.

Each time a car turned through that final corner, Frankie kept looking for the fateful oil spill that would hopefully send Grandad spiralling out of control. But lap after lap the oil spill failed to appear.

'Grandad,' Frankie asked, 'you don't happen to know when the oil got spilt on the track do you?'

'Of course not,' Grandad barked, like a dog at a kite show. 'If I knew that I would have avoided it in the first place.'

'Of course,' Frankie mumbled.

He felt uneasy and very, very weird, which is not surprising, considering that this was undoubtedly the single strangest moment in the life of Frankie Fish. Here he was, sitting in the grandstand of a car race that happened many decades before he was born, watching his grandad (whom he was ALSO sitting next to!) race a car that he hoped would crash.

It was even weirder than the day the Yo-Yo Team came to school to perform tricks and ended up sparking a gastro outbreak. (Long story with too many yucky images to go into here.)

As the cheers and jeers in the stands got louder, Frankie noticed Grandad's eyes were shut tighter than ever before, like he was bracing himself for the impact.

'It's the final lap of the Big Race,' the commentator screamed excitedly, *'and it's Alfie Fish, a quarter of a lap in front of his arch nemesis, Clancy Fairplay. What a famous victory this will be ...'*

The frenzied crowd got to their feet to cheer their heroes home. But Frankie's eyes were fixed on that one corner, which was still missing an oil spill.

What does this mean? Frankie thought, anxiously touching his face, which luckily at least *felt* normal.

At that exact same moment, the clouds that had been threatening to spill all day let loose.

The heavens opened up as rain tumbled down onto the crowd and the track. The crowd barely noticed, though, as they continued yelling and screaming as if they were competing with the engines of the magnificent cars.

But then the commentator's tone changed from excited to cautious.

'Hold on a moment, folks ... the rain is pouring onto the track. Visibility out there must be almost zero. This could sound the death knell for a driver. Hometown hero Alfie Fish is approaching now. The officials should stop the race –'

But it was far too late to stop anything because Alfie Fish was now heading to the final corner. Water sprayed up from his tyres like he had fire hoses under the back of his car.

The crowd ooohed and ahhhed at this latest twist as the commentator continued.

'*Well, Alfie Fish is approaching that final corner, showing no signs of slowing down. In fact, he seems to be waving to the crowd. Let's hope he is keeping at least one eye on the road as he takes the corner and –*'

The crowd suddenly stopped cheering, and held its collective breath.

For Frankie, everything went into slow motion: the crowd waving curled-up race programs, Grandad's car moving towards the final corner, even the rain pelting down on the track seemed to be descending at a warped speed. Frankie looked at Grandad, who was gripping the Sonic Suitcase and staring down at his own lap, his teeth clenched.

Frankie put his hands over his eyes and peeped through the cracks between his fingers as Grandad's car spun out of control and slammed hard into the wall.

CRASH!

Frankie felt like he hadn't taken a breath in days. The crowd was eerily silent as debris from Grandad's car was flung out across the track. The silence was only broken by Frankie Fish, who jumped on his seat and screamed ...

'YEEEEEEESSSSSSSSSSS!!!!!!!!' with both hands stretched out into the air.

Grandad's eyes suddenly opened as he quickly got to his feet and saw his crashed blue racecar on the side of the track.

'YEEEEESSSSSSS!!!!' he also screamed with joy to the utter confusion of those around him.

'Have some decency,' the lady in front with a dead fox draped over her shoulders snapped.

'Of course,' Grandad said apologetically. 'I guess that probably did seem a little ... ah ... inappropriate.' But when the woman turned away, he pulled Frankie into a hug – the very first they'd ever had.

'We did it,' Frankie said, his voice muffled.

'We *did*, lad.'

There was the sound of Clancy Fairplay's car roaring as it successfully navigated the final corner, taking the winner's chequered flag. A moment later, paramedics sprinted onto the track, carrying medical bags and a stretcher.

'Are you OK?' asked Frankie, peering at the car heap for a glimpse of Young Alfie. A stomach-dropping thought had just occurred to him. *What if Grandad actually dies this time instead of just losing his hand?* There had been enough disruption to the time path that anything was possible.

'I'm not sure,' replied Grandad, sounding like the same thought had just occurred to him too.

Frankie grimaced as he watched Clancy Fairplay pump his fists from the safety of his car. *More like Clancy Lowlife*, thought Frankie, disgusted. *What a sad and ungracious jerk that guy is.*

Then he felt his grandad tugging on his sleeve.

'Frankie. *Look*.' Grandad's voice was hoarse and urgent.

Frankie turned to see the old man, grey-faced, staring at his right hand. Except that the hand wasn't there anymore. In its place was the hook Frankie had always known.

We've done it! thought Frankie.

But his triumph faded when only a second later the hook flickered once, twice, and his grandad's hand reappeared.

Frankie froze, his eyes round. 'Hang on. If your hand is flickering, that means the protective force field is fading. Which means –'

Grandad glanced up at Frankie and almost jumped out of his seat. 'Your face!' he cried.

Frankie clutched his cheeks. 'What? What's happening?'

Grandad snatched a little mirror from the lady sitting next to him, who was fixing her make-up, and shoved it in front of Frankie's face. 'Look!'

Frankie couldn't believe what – or who – he was staring at. He didn't see his own reflection … but the ghost of a freckly boy with red hair. As he watched, horrified, the boy turned into a girl with long blonde hair, who morphed into a boy with a mohawk, who transformed into a boy with glasses, and so on.

'**Aaaarrgghh!!**' screamed Frankie, like an arachnophobe at a *Spider-Man* premiere. 'My face!'

'It's just puberty, dear,' the lady said, snatching her mirror back.

'You should have seen how my Hamish looked at your age.'

'Nobody told me puberty involved my face morphing from boy to girl!' Frankie was freaking out. 'Why has it turned my face on shuffle?'

'I don't know for sure,' muttered Grandad as he dragged Frankie towards the exit, 'but perhaps the time continuum is confused.' He spun Frankie around to examine his face(s) again. 'Or maybe ... maybe it's preparing for a world without Frankie Fish.'

CHAPTER 18

TiME QUiCKLY TiCKS AWAY

'Coming through, coming through!' yelled a paramedic as he helped carry a stretcher through St Mary's emergency corridor. 'We have the runner-up of the Big Race here, Alfie Fish! He's in a stable but critical condition, and we're going to need the surgeon down here stat ... '

The paramedics whooshed past Grandad Alfie and Frankie, who had just arrived at the hospital.

Frankie turned his back momentarily, fearful he might somehow upset the time quantum, or the universe's gravitational pull, or some other thing he didn't quite understand. Also, he was embarrassed about his face(s).

'How do I look?' Frankie asked Grandad, understandably feeling a little self-conscious.

'Hideous,' Grandad said, 'but at least your face has stopped changing.'

Frankie glared at him.

'OK then, grumpy bum,' Grandad said. 'Let's go keep Clancy away from your nanna until she goes into my surgery, and then we can get out of here.'

It didn't take them long to find Nurse Mavis Hopley. As doctors and nurses whirled around, she was carefully and quickly looking over young Alfie Fish, who was passed out on the stretcher. The scene was chaotic, but Nurse Hopley was the definition of grace under pressure. When everyone was ready, she helped wheel the injured racing-car driver and her future husband (um ... hopefully) into the emergency ward.

'She's like an angel caught in a daydream,' Grandad murmured.

Frankie looked around for an industrial-strength vomit bag.

Before Grandad had the chance to offer up more poetic reflections on his future wife (... um, hopefully), he was interrupted by ... guess who?

If you said King Jerk, the jerkiest jerk in all of Jerksville, Clancy Fairplay, then you would be right.

'Is Nurse Hopley in the vicinity? Mavis Hopley?' he bellowed smarmily. In one hand he held his winner's cup. His cologne wafted up the corridor, a curious combination of gasoline and sleaze. Grandad and Frankie were too late.

'Clancy Fairplay, the stupid, arrogant fool,' Grandad muttered. Frankie clutched at his sleeve, holding him back.

Nurse Hopley turned around to see who was hollering after her.

'May I help you, Mr Fairplay?' asked Nurse Hopley, a little flustered.

'Miss Mavis,' Clancy began pompously. 'As I'm sure you know, I won the Big Race today fair and square, no matter what anybody may say. As a result, and in line with our agreement, I was hoping you would do me the honour ...'

Frankie watched anxiously. He knew he should just let this play out and hope Nanna made the right decision to kick this jerk to the curb, but after everything that had happened today, he was worried about leaving anything to fate. But what could he do?

Meanwhile, Clancy Fairplay continued to remind everyone (especially Mavis Hopley) that he'd won the Big Race today.

'And as such, it's only right that you honour your commitment and accompany me on a date, Miss Mavis, right this instant!'

Clancy evidently thought this was a romantic and not-at-all-rude statement.

Nurse Hopley looked a little perturbed.

'Well, that is very nice of you to think of me so quickly after winning the Big Race, but I have a patient who needs urgent care at the moment.'

'You mean old Stinky Fathead Fish?' said Clancy, rolling his eyes. 'He'll be OK, just a little banged up is all. You *did* promise ...' He was clearly getting annoyed that Mavis Hopley was not throwing herself at his feet.

Inspired, Frankie darted into the room, leaving Grandad to follow. 'Excuse me, Mr Fairplay,' he blurted. 'Can I get a selfie? Er ... I mean, an autograph?'

Clancy spun around, bright red. So much smoke came out of his ears that a nearby Nurse Gretchen thought his brain might have actually exploded.

'I don't do AUTOGRAPHS!' he hissed in Frankie's face.

'Oh come on, I'm just a kid,' said Frankie, making his eyes wide and hopeful.

This seemed to infuriate Clancy. 'I hate kids!!' he yelled loudly, like he was screaming in the middle of a cyclone. It echoed around the corridors of the hospital.

Nurse Hopley took a step back, disgusted. 'You don't like children? What kind of monster doesn't like *children?*'

Clancy Fairplay immediately realised what he had done, and his face almost morphed like Frankie's. Clancy went from Angry-Jerk face to Whoops-I-Shouldn't-Have-Done-That face.

It was time for the finishing touch. Frankie reached out and tugged at Clancy's sleeve. 'Please, mister. Can I ...?'

'Get away from me!' screamed Clancy, swinging at Frankie with his winner's cup. As Frankie ducked, Nurse Mavis's eyes widened with horror.

'How *dare* you treat that innocent lad like that, you pompous rat?' she yelled, like she too was now in a cyclone. 'Get out of this hospital this instant!'

'But you promised me a date,' Clancy protested weakly.

'I wouldn't date you even if it turned out you could poop gold,' Nurse Mavis snapped. **'Now SCRAM.'**

With that, Clancy slunk away like the loser he really was.

Nurse Hopley laid a hand on Frankie's shoulder. 'I'm sorry I yelled at him so loudly but I don't know – I just feel very protective of you for some reason,' she said, apologetically. 'Are you OK, young man?'

Frankie pretended to wipe away some tears, just for good measure. 'I am now,' he said, 'but what a bully. I can't imagine why *anyone* would *ever* want to date *him*.'

'I could never date a man who hated children,'

declared Mavis. 'Now, is there anything I can do for you?' she added with the tenderness of a saint.

Frankie shook his head, but then remembered there was one thing. 'Will Grand– will Alfie Fish be OK, do you think?' he asked.

Nurse Hopley sighed, and said, 'He's going to lose his hand, but I think he'll live. He's a fighter, that man.'

'And very handsome too, don't you think?' added Grandad, hopefully.

Nurse Mavis laughed despite herself. 'Well yes, yes he is,' she agreed, her cheeks a little pink. 'Now off home with the both of you.'

And that's exactly what Frankie and Grandad tried to do …

… But I did say *tried*, didn't I?

CHAPTER 19

THE SHORT, SAD LiFE OF A BATTERY

Frankie ushered Grandad down the hospital corridor and found an empty ward. Closing the door behind them, Frankie moved purposefully to the empty bed and opened the Sonic Suitcase on top of it.

'Now that we know Young Alfie is OK,' he said urgently, 'we need to get home before the protective force field collapses altogether. Let's move!'

Grandad moved Frankie out of the way and started typing into the Sonic Suitcase. 'Exactly how many time-travel shows have you seen, kiddo?'

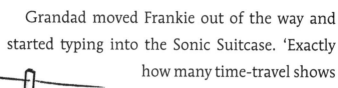

There wasn't time to go through exactly how many movies or episodes or books or games! 'Just trust me. If we don't get home quick-sticks, it could be disastrous.'

'Define *disastrous*,' Grandad asked, still typing.

'Well, we might disappear off the face of the earth forever, or we could get lost in time and space for all eternity,' said Frankie.

He scratched an itch on his cheek, which had started morphing again, and felt stubble.

'Yep, that's the textbook definition of *disastrous*, all right,' Grandad said, gulping. Then he glanced up at Frankie, shock written across his face.

'What now? I have a beard, don't I,' said Frankie, searching the room for a mirror.

'That's not the worst of it,' replied Grandad, his face pale. 'We're out of battery.'

His wrinkly hands trembling, Grandad turned the Sonic Suitcase around so that Frankie could see it for his own eyes (which were currently those of a brown-eyed girl with lashes to die for).

Frankie saw the battery reading as clear as the D- on his last Biology project.

Three. Lousy. Per cent.

'What per cent do we need to get back to 2017 again?' Frankie asked Grandad, his throat dry.

'Seventeen,' Grandad replied. His face was unreadable.

'So we find a generator or something,' said Frankie, his face suddenly snapping back to his own. 'Charge it up again and get out of here.'

'It's 1952, Frankie,' Grandad groaned. 'We can't just plug the Sonic Suitcase into a power point – the voltage is all wrong and it could destroy the suitcase altogether. We need a strong, pure electric charge!'

'What are you saying, Grandad?' Frankie pleaded.

Grandad buried his face in his hands. 'I don't think there's anything we can do, kiddo. It's over. The only way we could generate enough electricity would be to somehow harness a bolt of *lightning* – which is basically impossible.'

Frankie leaned heavily against the wall. 'So after all that – we've saved the family in 2017, but now we're stuck in 1952?'

'I'm afraid so,' Grandad whispered. 'Unless we can find a natural source of electricity, Frankie, it may just be ... the end.'

If Frankie Fish's life were a movie, this is the moment where you'd hear a sudden *strum of guitar*.

Frankie lifted his head, his eyes wide. 'What did you just say?'

'I said ... um ... I don't remember. What did I say?' Grandad replied, which kind of ruined the moment a little.

'You said "unless we can find a natural source of electricity",' his grandson reminded him.

A second strum of the guitar.

'If you say so,' Grandad muttered.

Frankie reached into his pocket and pulled out the piece of yellow paper he had put in there, all those years in the future. He unfolded it and gave it to Grandad triumphantly.

'What's this?' Grandad said.

'You tell me,' Frankie said.

Grandad stared at Frankie, his face blank. 'Um, wasn't it where I took Nanna on our first date?'

'Yes … and now, where was it?' asked Frankie, pointing his finger at the print that read *The Amazing Freido*.

Grandad smiled. 'Was it Timezone?'

Guitar crashes out of tune a little.

'What? No! How do you even know about Timezone?' said Frankie, both confused and impressed. 'No, you took Nanna to see this magician, the Amazing Freido.'

'Don't remember,' said Grandad with a shrug. 'Was he any good?'

'No idea, but I do know the big trick he finished on,' said Frankie meaningfully.

'He made all the boogers in the world disappear?' asked Grandad.

Frankie rolled his eyes. 'Oh my God, **NO**. His big finish was *The Water Tank of Death* – and guess what was **IN** the Water Tank of Death?'

'… Dead people?' asked Grandad.

'**EELS!**' Frankie yelled, forgetting they were in a hospital. '*Electric* eels!'

'What's your point, kid?' Grandad barked. 'Are you just going to name animals? I can do that too. Lions, anteaters, wombats, sharks ... um, have I said lions already?'

Frankie thought he might burst. 'Grandad, if we can get to the day of the Amazing Freido's Magic Show, we could use the charge off the electric eels to get the Sonic Suitcase back up to seventeen per cent!' he said in a rush.

Grandad went very still. Then he brightened. 'That's crazy. Brilliant, but crazy.'

Frankie's knees were feeling very wobbly. 'I *know* it's crazy, but it's the only plan we've got! Tell me – is three lousy per cent enough to get us one week into the future, to the night of your first date?'

Grandad thought hard, his eyes sharper now. 'It should be. If we're very careful ...'

'So, all we need to do,' Frankie thought aloud, pacing back and forth like a detective solving a mystery, 'is plug an electric eel into our time computer. Grandad, by any chance, does your time computer have a port for an electric eel?'

'I don't think so,' replied Grandad, 'but if we could just get some copper wire to transfer the electric charge from the eel to the Sonic Suitcase –'

'Easier said than done, old man, this isn't a TV show,' said Frankie, shaking his head. Then he exclaimed, 'Oh my God, that's it!'

'What's it?' asked Grandad, looking a bit muddled again.

'We need to find a TV,' said Frankie, with the biggest grin we've seen since chapter one.

CHAPTER 20

TWO PER CENT

The Sonic Suitcase had officially gone down to two per cent and Grandad and Frankie were now officially in a rush. The kind of rush your dad gets in when he's running late to the big game and he can't find his lucky jocks, but multiplied by a thousand.

Now, televisions were still pretty new in 1952, but Frankie was confident of finding one. For one thing, they were much harder to hide than 2017 models. They were larger and boxier, with amplifiers, lamps, photo-electric cells, arc lights, transmitters, lenses, and lots and lots of **WIRES**.

The plan was to take some copper wiring from the back of a 1952 TV set and somehow use it to get an electric charge from the Amazing Freido's eels to charge the time computer and get the two of them home. It was crazy, it was brilliant – and there was every chance it wouldn't work.

But first things first: the TV. Frankie managed to locate one in a special ward on the top floor of St Mary's, and took some copper wiring out of the back of it, following Grandad's instructions. He thought it was going to be much tougher to do than it actually was, but the patients watching had just taken their medication and were snoring louder than an elephant with a megaphone.

Clutching the copper wiring, Frankie sprinted

back into their hospital room. Grandad was frantically tapping away at the Sonic Suitcase, setting up their co-ordinates for the short jump.

'I have no idea if this is going to work,' he mumbled.

'Then we should go to plan B,' said Frankie.

Grandad looked hopeful. 'We have a plan B?'

'Yep, it's exactly the same as plan A. Plan C, D and E are the same too, for that matter.'

Grandad mumbled something else, but this time it was under his breath and involved some very creative swearing, so Frankie didn't bother asking him to repeat it.

For all his grumbling though, Grandad knew just as well as Frankie that they were running out of options *and* time. Frankie's face had begun changing again, more frequently than a lion tamer changes his/her undies, and that was enough for Grandad to move into full throttle mode – which, when you are eighty-five, is tougher than you'd think.

As the old man finalised the co-ordinates, Frankie kept watch at the door, his feet tapping nervously. The last thing they needed was for another person to get caught up in their hectic time-warping adventure. He stared through the little window out into the hospital corridor, thoughts stirring in his mind like the soup in Nanna Fish's enormous pot.

Then it was Frankie's turn to have serious doubts about plans A, B, C, D and E. 'Grandad,' he said worriedly. 'What happens if we get to the Amazing Freido and for some reason, you haven't asked Nanna out, or maybe you did but she said no, or perhaps she changed her mind about Clancy Fairplay?' Frankie's heart was racing. 'Way too much has changed, so how can we know for sure that everything will turn out OK?'

Grandad stopped typing for a moment, and sighed. 'It's a fair point, kiddo. If I've learned anything from you today, it's that we *can't* trust time, and we can't trust that we haven't messed it all up.'

Frankie waited, unsure whether Grandad had finished making his point, which, if he *had* finished, seemed a little pointless.

Luckily, Grandad went on. 'I guess the only thing we can trust is the love between your grandad and your nanna.'

This time Frankie didn't reach for a vomit vessel. Deep down, he knew it was the only hope they had left.

Grandad held a hand out to Frankie. 'So come on ... Let's go see a magic show.'

With that, and without any certainty that

two per cent battery was enough to get them anywhere, it was time to go. Frankie came over and held tight to the suitcase's handle.

Grandad murmured, 'Happy travels.'

And like that, they disappeared from St Mary's Hospital.

CHAPTER 21

THE NOT-SO-
AMAZING FREIDO

R ain, rotting fish and old newspapers. They were the first impressions Frankie had when they arrived in a dark cobblestoned alleyway.

Frankie didn't feel quite as jet lagged as last time, maybe because of the short distance. Then he realised he was alone. 'Grandad?' he called into the cold night air.

There was a sudden thumping from inside a nearby dumpster, and then someone swore loudly. A moment later, Grandad stood up, a banana peel draped over his bald spot. 'Blasted computer,' he grunted, throwing it off. 'Happy travels my bare bum!'

'Where are we?' asked Frankie, trying manfully to suppress a giggle.

Grandad looked around, then pointed triumphantly at a sign: **STAGE DOOR**.

'That's the George Theatre, where your nanna and I saw Freido perform,' beamed Grandad. 'Not too bad for an old fart, am I?'

'You did land in a garbage dump,' Frankie snickered.

Luckily his grandad didn't seem to hear. 'Help me out of this bin, lad,' he said, 'and let's see if he's there.'

STAGE
DOOR

The Amazing Freido was a sixty-three-year-old magician who – despite having supposedly sent people into outer space in an elaborately decorated Space Coffin – had never actually left Scotland. Even so, Freido was a showman, and a decent magician. The George Theatre was half-full for tonight's performance (or half-empty, depending on how you view life).

At that moment, Freido was conducting his final safety-check on the Water Tank of Death. Heaven forbid if the Water Tank of Death wasn't safe, right? But his inspection was rudely interrupted by a knocking on the stage door.

'Clarissa!' he screamed. 'Answer that blasted door and get rid of whoever's there!'

There was no answer from Clarissa.

The Amazing Freido let out an exaggerated huff that was straight out of drama school as he descended from the stepladder and stomped over to the stage door.

A peculiar sight was awaiting him on the

other side: a young boy wearing bizarre clothes and an old man with a face like a sucked lemon. The old man went to speak, but the boy jumped in first.

'Good evening, sir. My grandad here really needs to use the bathroom so that **HE CAN DO AN URGENT POOP**.'

Grandad's cheeks immediately turned a deep, shiny red. The boy, of course, was Frankie, and inside he was cheering, *YES! PAYBACK!!*

'I'm afraid **NOBODY** is allowed backstage with the Amazing Freido,' replied the Amazing Freido in his magnificently deep voice, which was perfectly complemented by a twirl of his cape.

'Please, please, **PLEASE?**' Frankie said, barely containing his grin. 'He's really busting, aren't you, Grandad?'

There was no grin detectable on Grandad's face whatsoever. 'I guess so,' he muttered.

'Why can't you use the toilets in the foyer like everyone else?' bellowed Freido.

'Please sir, we are big fans,' Frankie pleaded. 'We've travelled so far to see you!'

'How far exactly?' asked Freido, preening a little.

'A whole week,' Grandad chimed in, 'just to see you.'

The Amazing Freido was flattered. 'OK fine, but be quick and don't piddle on the tiles,' he said grandly, ushering them inside. 'I may be the world's greatest magician, but some things cannot be erased.' (Piddle definitely can be.)

Grandad squirmed as he slunk off to the bathroom to have a pretend wee/poop and Frankie smirked to himself.

Frankie 1. Grandad 1.

But Frankie didn't gloat for long. He had work to do. 'Everyone says your live show is amazing,' he lied hastily as the Amazing Freido started walking back to the Water Tank of Death. 'I've seen all your clips on YouTube –'

The Amazing Freido stopped. 'YouTube? What is a YouTube?'

Frankie panicked slightly. 'Um ... well ... I just think you're amazing?'

'They don't call me the Amazing Freido for no reason,' replied Freido modestly, even though nobody had called him that – he'd chosen the name himself in a cafe in Glasgow.

'Wow! I can't wait to see the Water Tank of Death,' said Frankie. 'How many eels are in there?'

'There are *six*,' replied Freido proudly.

'Awesome. And are they big?' Frankie asked excitedly.

'The biggest in the Loch. The largest one is the size of your arm, laddie. Bruno is his name. He's particularly angry today so he may sit this show out, but don't worry, his brothers have plenty of zip.'

'And they are definitely electric eels, aren't they?' Frankie pressed. 'Like your flyer says?'

'Of course they are!' the magician zapped back proudly. 'It wouldn't be much of a trick if they were just regular eels.'

'**Wooooooooow,**' said Frankie again, laying it on extra thick. 'You know, I want to become a magician one day, but I don't have anyone amazing like you to learn from. Maybe you could do us the honour of allowing my grandad and me to watch your show from backstage?'

Frankie felt his voice shudder a little, like when he'd asked his dad if he could go on holidays with Drew Bird.

'Not a chance,' the Amazing Freido said firmly. 'The only people allowed back here are myself and Clarissa, my beautiful yet recently lacking-in-attention-to-detail assistant.'

With perfect timing Frankie heard a voice as sweet as an angel: 'Awwwww! You have a fan, Freido!'

Frankie's jaw dropped. Walking towards him was possibly the most beautiful woman he had ever seen. Her legs were those of an Olympic high jumper and her red hair flowed down her back like a waterless hairy waterfall. Her eyes were as blue as the water in the Water Tank of Death, but far less threatening. The sequins on her dress shone and shimmered like a meteor shower. Looking at this lady was like looking at something so good it made your eyes hurt. Like a bowl of ice-cream resting on a cloud of fairy floss.

'Ah, Clarissa,' said the Amazing Freido. 'Decided to turn up, did you?'

Despite the sarcasm, the Amazing Freido softened slightly in Clarissa's presence. It quickly became clear that there were two men in love with Clarissa in the backstage room.

Then Grandad returned from the bathroom. 'Ahem,' he said, as he laid eyes on Clarissa in her feathered headdress. Now there were three men in love with Clarissa.

'Clarissa, please escort these two outside,' instructed the Amazing Freido. 'I can't have any distractions backstage.'

'But they are *soooo* cute,' Clarissa gushed. 'Go on, let them stay, you old fool.'

The Amazing Freido fake-laughed through gritted teeth. 'Come now, Clarissa. First you arrive late and now you won't ...'

Suddenly, Clarissa's warm smile – that only moments earlier had reminded Frankie of springtime – turned as cold as a polar bear's refrigerator. Her eyes bored into Freido.

'The reason I was late, Amazing Freido, is because I was ironing your handkerchiefs.' This time it was *her* teeth that were gritted. 'And unless ironing is a magic trick you want to learn, I suggest you let these two gentlemen stay here for the show.'

The Amazing Freido paused, obviously weighing up the thought of ironing his own handkerchiefs, then let out the fakest laugh heard this side of 1952.

'Hahahahaha ... I guess I can make an exception just this once.'

Frankie shot Grandad a grin. 'Thanks, Amazing Freido! Just one more question.

Are you *definitely* doing the Water Tank of Death trick with the eels tonight?' he asked.

'Of course,' Clarissa interrupted. 'That's our big showstopper! In fact, it was *my* idea ...'

'OK, that's enough,' Freido jumped in, rudely cutting Clarissa off. 'Now, if you two scoundrels are staying back here, stand in that corner over there and keep out of our way.

Clarissa, keep an eye on them.'

Clarissa sighed loudly, and rolled her eyes.

Frankie and Grandad dutifully went and stood in the corner next to the curtain, as Clarissa checked her make-up and Freido preened his moustache. The Water Tank of Death stood between them, covered loosely with a long, slippery black cloth.

'Are they there yet?' Frankie asked worriedly.

'Who?'

'You and Nanna Fish!'

'Oh.'

Grandad peeked through a tiny gap in the curtain, searching through the theatre for the two young lovebirds.

'Anything?' Frankie hissed.

'No,' said Grandad, hollowly.

Frankie peeked through the gap too.

Right there in the front row, where Alfie and Mavis were supposed to be sitting, were two empty seats. **NOT** a good sign.

Frankie felt a knot in his tummy the size of a football. He knew his grandad and nanna had to sit down and watch the show if they were to become his grandad and nanna.

The plan was suddenly looking shakier than a bowl of jelly in a jumping castle.

CHAPTER 22

LET'S GET EEL

One of the few things Frankie had learned from his Biology project was that electric eels actually *do* give off electricity. It's how they got their name. If they gave off a foul stench they would've probably been called stinky eels. But one of the many things Frankie *didn't* know about electric eels was exactly how much electricity they produced. He hoped more than he'd ever hoped for anything that it would be enough to recharge the Sonic Suitcase's battery back up to seventeen per cent, so that they could get home before Frankie disappeared off the face of the earth.

Suddenly, the lights in the George Theatre were switched off, and a drumroll sounded from behind the curtains. A single spotlight shone onto the middle of the red curtain, and the Amazing Freido's extravaganza began.

'**Ladies and Gentlemen!**' the Amazing Freido bellowed into a microphone from backstage. 'He has wowed them in **New York City!**' (He hadn't.) 'He amazed them in **Tokyo!**' (Never been there.) 'And they just couldn't get enough of him in **Barcelona!**' (He had paella once.) 'Now back in his hometown of **Glasgow** ...' (He had actually never left.) 'It's **THE AMAZING FREIDO!**'

Grand music rang out as the Amazing Freido put the microphone down and appeared through the red curtain with a flourish. He twirled his cape as he bowed to the enthusiastic applause. A moment later, he was joined by his beautiful assistant Clarissa.

As soon as the show got started, so did Frankie and Grandad. They hustled over to the Water Tank of Death with the Sonic Suitcase and their bundle of copper wires.

With sweaty hands, Frankie tugged on the slippery black cloth. It slithered off, revealing the enormous tank. Around the base was a kind of black skirt, and beneath that was a small ledge, just big enough for a Frankie-sized kid to lie on.

Grandad laid the Sonic Suitcase on the ledge and began carefully, but quickly, connecting the copper wiring to the complex machinery inside.

'Hurry!' hissed Frankie. 'Before someone sees us.'

The Amazing Freido may not have been world-famous, but he knew his magic and performed it well. With Clarissa expertly twirling and prancing around him, the Amazing Freido did the classics. A rabbit jumped from his hat, an extraordinarily long line of brightly coloured and impeccably ironed handkerchiefs slipped from his sleeve, doves fluttered out from beneath a white tablecloth. The crowd oohed and aahed and applauded, which the Amazing Freido lapped up like a thirsty horse.

Meanwhile, on the side of the stage, the time-travellers were still racing to get their set-up sorted. Grandad fiddled with the wires as Frankie ran back and forth to the little hole in the curtain – but the two seats in the front row stayed empty. Where were Young Alfie Fish and Nurse Hopley? Had Frankie and Grandad's interfering disrupted history forever? After Clancy Fairplay's atrocious reaction to Frankie, had Nurse Hopley decided she didn't **EVER** want to be around any racecar drivers? It was almost too painful to consider.

Frankie ran to a backstage mirror that was surrounded by flowers (sent to the Amazing Freido *by* the Amazing Freido). He anxiously checked his face under the bright lights, and was horrified to see he now had peroxide-white hair and a six-centimetre scar down his left cheek.

As the oohs and aahs continued from the audience, Frankie sunk to the floor. The fact that his face was still changing could only mean one thing: the plan was failing. Frankie suddenly felt swamped with despair. He wouldn't ever get home. **Not EVER**. It was pointless to keep trying. He may as well just sit here and wait until he disappeared.

As Frankie's eyes began filling with tears, he reached into his pocket for a tissue, but all he found were some dried-out flowers.

Frankie stared at them, a tingle going down

his spine. They were the forgotten forget-me-nots that Nanna had given him so many years into the future. Frankie could almost see Nanna as if she was standing right there in front of him with her sweet warm smile, the smell of her blueberry pancakes filling his nostrils.

Suddenly, his mum and dad were right there with him too, joined by his sister Saint Lou. *Please don't give up, Francis!* he imagined Lou saying. *You're the only one who can fix this terrible situation.*

Imaginary Lou had a much less annoying voice than the real Saint Lou. And for the first time ever she sounded like she was depending on him. Like the entire Fish family was.

Very Big Guitar Strum.

Frankie jumped to his feet, his batteries recharged. Now he just needed to do the same to the Sonic Suitcase.

Frankie slid across to Grandad like a baseball player sliding into home base.

'This is going to work, Grandad,' Frankie promised as Grandad finally took the other end of the copper wire and wrapped it around a small bolt.

'It'd better,' replied Grandad, not looking certain at all. 'Now all we have to do is get this bolt into the tank, and then –'

All of a sudden the lights flickered. The crowd gasped nervously as the sound of thunder filled the room.

Backstage, Frankie and Grandad froze as they heard the light tip-tapping of footsteps approaching.

Frankie yanked the wire out of Grandad's hands and tossed it into the water, where the bolt sank slowly to the bottom of the tank. The wire glinted in the low light, but neither Grandad or Frankie were around to see it. Grandad dived to the side of the stage, and Frankie ducked under the Water Tank of Death just as Clarissa appeared.

That was close, Frankie gasped to himself. He felt the wheels below him start to roll, and realised that Clarissa was pushing the tank onstage.

'And now,' the Amazing Freido announced, 'I shall perform a trick that no-one in the history of the world has ever attempted, not even the great Houdini.' (Not true – he did this most nights.) 'My beautiful assistant Clarissa shall handcuff and blindfold me. She will then usher me into a tank full of water. But not just **ANY** tank! This is the **WORLD-FAMOUS WATER TANK OF DEATH**.' (Nobody outside of Scotland had heard of it.) 'And then, ladies and gentleman, Clarissa shall release not one, not two, not four, but **FIVE** electric eels inside the tank!'

Beneath the tank's skirt, Frankie squeezed his eyes shut and crossed his fingers. This HAD to work.

The sound of thunder was booming through-out the theatre.

'They say if a man receives more than five attacks from an electric eel *he shall DIE*!' proclaimed the Amazing Freido. (This fact is not completely factual – but as you'll know by now, both facts *and* magic tricks were just an illusion for Freido.)

'Bring out the Water Tank of Death!' shouted Freido, as Clarissa rolled it out right on cue. Under the flickering stage lights, the Water Tank of Death looked quite dramatic to unsuspecting eyes – even though it was just a regular tank with lightning bolts drawn on either side in gold paint with a black paint trim.

Speaking of unsuspecting eyes, neither Clarissa nor Freido had noticed the copper wiring connected to the back of the Water Tank of Death, leading down to the Sonic Suitcase – and Frankie – beneath the tank. Cautiously, Frankie lifted up one edge of the tank's skirt and looked out at the side of the stage. Grandad was standing there, his knuckles crammed into his mouth. Frankie knew what he was thinking.

It'll be a miracle if they don't see it, and if they do – it's game over.

Frankie quickly dropped the cloth as the Amazing Freido climbed a small ladder into the deadly tank, which, despite its name, had so far been responsible for zero deaths. 'It's nice, once you're in,' Freido quipped, as Clarissa made a show of blindfolding and handcuffing him. It was clear that this was her favourite part of the show.

'Now, Clarissa,' Freido boomed, 'fetch the Electric Eels!'

Frankie reached over to the Sonic Suitcase. The battery life ticked down to one per cent. 'Hurry, hurry ...' he whispered.

Cue more flashing lights and sounds of thunder as Clarissa fetched a bucket of electric eels from the back of the stage. But as Clarissa walked back towards the Tank of Death, she noticed something that stopped her in her tracks: a suspicious, long copper wire leading from inside the water, all the way under the curtain at the tank's base – out of which poked a twelve-year-old's feet.

CHAPTER 23

CLARISSA'S REVENGE

'CLARISSA!!!' screamed the Amazing Freido from the Water Tank of Death. 'Are you deaf or just completely unprofessional?' The slightly baffled audience looked at each other, trying to work out if Freido's belligerence towards his assistant was real or just part of the show.

Clarissa stood with the bucket of eels looking at Freido waist deep in room-temperature water.

Then she looked at the pair of feet under the tank.

Then Clarissa did the unexpected. Perhaps because she was tired of being referred to as the Amazing Freido's 'beautiful' assistant, or maybe because she had a soft spot for pranks – Clarissa gave Grandad a small nod and a smile, and gently nudged Frankie on the feet. It was the kind of nudge that meant, '*Don't worry. I won't dob.*' Then, without a word, she continued onto the ladder of the Water Tank of Death, where a soggy Freido was growing increasingly impatient, and emptied the eels into the tank.

Splash. Splash. Splash. Splash. Splash.

As the audience oohed and ahhed again, and the Amazing Freido began to struggle out of his binding, Frankie scrambled out from under the tank's skirt and commando-crawled across the back of the stage to Grandad.

'If we don't get out of here, you should marry that woman,' gasped Grandad to his grandson, who wasn't about to disagree. 'Just keep your fingers crossed. Remember, each charge only goes for two milliseconds and I estimate we need at least five charges to get our battery back up over seventeen per cent ... which will hopefully be enough to get us back home.'

The time-travellers watched anxiously as the five electric eels swam around in the Water Tank of Death. The blindfolded Amazing Freido wasn't having much luck with his handcuffs, or perhaps that was all part of the show? Hard to tell.

Frankie wasn't quite sure where to look, but he stared intently at the copper wire, hoping to see some kind of electric charge move along it into the Sonic Suitcase. Nothing.

The crowd was really getting into the act now, cheering and gasping as the eels circled the flailing magician. If only they knew what else was happening on that stage – that there was a twelve-year-old boy and his grandad from the future hiding behind the curtain, trying to charge up their crazy homemade time machine to hurl them back to 2017.

Or that if the blushing couple who were *supposed* to be sitting in the front row didn't arrive soon and seal their love for each other, then an entire family of Fishes could become as extinct as dinosaurs or fax machines.

But of course, the crowd knew none of this. They just knew that the Amazing Freido was thrashing about in a water tank of electric eels and, truth be told, they were on the eels' side.

'Bite him in the private parts!' yelled one Glaswegian from the back, as the crowd became rowdy with excitement.

'Ouch!' Freido screamed, as an eel charged him.

'Yeeeaaahhhhh!!!!' screamed the crowd. And as they screamed, Frankie and Grandad let out their own shouts of delight – because just as Freido was being bitten by the first electric eel, a young Alfie Fish and his date, Mavis Hopley, walked arm-in-arm to their seats. They may have been running a little late, but for Frankie and Grandad, they were right on time.

BZZZZT!

'Yeeeaaahhhhh!!!!' yelled Frankie at the top of his lungs.

At exactly the same moment, a trail of electricity ran all the way from inside the Tank of Death, down the copper wiring and into the Sonic Suitcase.

'It's working!' Grandad exclaimed, grabbing Frankie's arm.

'Four more. We need at least four more!' Frankie whispered excitedly.

Another electric charge. **BZZZZT!**

'Aaargh!' screamed Freido as the audience broke out into rapturous applause.

'Three more!' Grandad breathed, almost cutting off the blood supply in Frankie's arm.

BZZZZT!

'Ouchy wah wah!!!' wailed Freido.

Even Clarissa gave a little yelp of excitement and discreetly punched a little air with her closed fist.

Wow, those eels were really going after Freido.

'*Two more*,' said Frankie and Grandad together.

The crowd was in a frenzy. 'Private parts! Private parts! Private parts!' chanted everyone in unison. The magic show was quickly turning into a WWE fight.

All of a sudden, Freido raised an arm towards the roof. He had gotten one hand free from the handcuffs. Surely the second one would be off very, very soon.

'Oh no,' said Frankie in a voice much louder than a whisper. 'He'll be out any second now. Did we get enough?'

Grandad's face fell, and he shook his head. 'It will take five charges *minimum* to get enough electricity into the computer,' he muttered. 'There have only been three.'

The crowd booed as the Amazing Freido triumphantly raised both hands and whipped off the blindfold. Some audience members were clearly hoping to see the very first death in the Water Tank of Death, but Freido had escaped – and was now gesturing grandly for his ladder out of the tank as more lightning and thunder effects filled the room. For some reason, the eels had decided to let him off easy now.

Frankie was frantic. Not caring if he was seen, he dived from the side of the stage and lifted the skirt of the tank to check the Sonic Suitcase. *Maybe Grandad's wrong*, he thought wildly. *Maybe we do have enough charge now ...*

But no. The suitcase only had thirteen per cent battery life, four short of what they needed.

Frankie looked back at Grandad, who was covering his face with his hands. Then he stared at the suitcase, forcing his brain to work harder than it ever had before.

Then he had an idea.

Bingo! Or rather... **BRUNO**.

The Amazing Freido had said the biggest eel, Bruno, was too angry to take part in today's performance. And Frankie knew that an angry electric eel was a powerful electric eel – and power was what they needed right now. Frankie looked over at the small tank that Clarissa had placed behind the Water Tank of Death and noticed it was rocking from side to side. Something very large and extremely furious was desperately trying to get out.

Frankie caught Clarissa's eye, then nodded towards the tank that held Bruno. Clarissa somehow understood and gave him a wink. Frankie decided right there and then he *would* marry her if this mission went awry.

Frankie sneaked over to the mini tank, cautiously opened the lid and was met with the biggest, angriest eel ever. Bruno's mouth opened wide like he was attempting to eat Frankie for lunch. Frankie fell back on his bum in fright as he saw electric charges shoot through the dark, swirling waters.

'Quick!' Grandad yelled as the Amazing Freido started climbing out of the Water Tank of Death. Frankie gritted his teeth. He picked up the mini tank and, with Bruno trying to take out a chunk of his arm, he threw the entire thing up towards Freido and into the Water Tank of Death.

'Nice Bruno,' the Amazing Freido whispered meekly.

The tank water instantly lit up like a wet Christmas tree. Frankie dived under the tank, getting a nice little shock himself in the process.

The Amazing Freido's hair went bolt upright, his pencil-thin moustache shot out at ninety degrees, and he went momentarily cross-eyed. The crowd gave him a standing ovation.

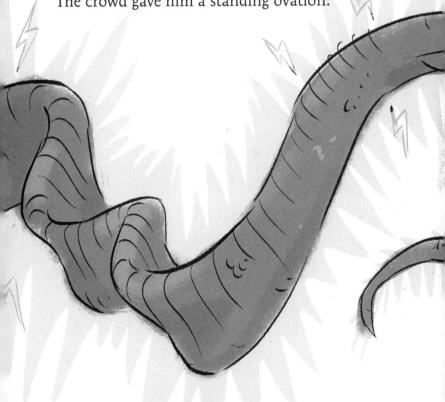

'Bruno!!!!' the Amazing Freido screamed as Clarissa giggled guiltily nearby.

Frankie looked up to see a spark of electricity flow from the Tank of Death into the now Suitcase of Life … and the battery ticked over from fourteen per cent to eighteen.

They'd done it!

Frankie turned triumphantly to Grandad and gave him a quick thumbs-up – aware that despite having a time machine, they still did not have much time at all.

As the Amazing Freido furiously – but gingerly – scrambled out of the Water Tank of Electricity, to the cheers of the delighted audience, Frankie snatched up the Sonic Suitcase and ran over to his grandad.

'Come on, Grandad. Let's go home!'

CHAPTER 24

TiME TO
GO HOME

Have you ever been stuck in a cramped, smelly toilet with your grandad? I do not recommend it, even in extraordinary circumstances such as these. Unfortunately, there was no other place at the George Theatre where Frankie and his grandad could activate the Sonic Suitcase without the danger of being seen.

Frankie swung the suitcase onto the cistern and Grandad immediately started typing in the co-ordinates. The little screen blinked and a message appeared. *Activate travel sequence?*

'OK, it's ready,' said Frankie, excitedly. 'Let's go, Grandad.'

But Grandad had a strange expression on his face. 'I think I might stay here,' he mumbled, to Frankie's horror.

'What? *Why?* We need to get back!' insisted Frankie.

Someone began pounding on the toilet door. 'Open up in there! I know it was you!' the Agitated Freido yelled. 'You could've killed me – in my own Water Tank of Death!'

'I like it here in the past,' Grandad said, ignoring the commotion. 'If I stay, I'll be able to see Mavis every day, and I can live among my memories.'

'But you don't belong here, Grandad. You need to come *now*!' pleaded Frankie, knowing it wouldn't take long for the battery's charge to slip below seventeen per cent again.

'But I'm scared,' whispered Grandad.

'Well, that makes two of us,' replied Frankie with a nervous smile.

'What happens if things have changed at home?' asked a suddenly frail-looking Alfie Fish.

'Well, to be honest I hope one thing *has* changed,' said Frankie.

'What's that?' asked Grandad.

Frankie squirmed, suddenly feeling bashful. 'I hope we're friends in the future, like the way we are in the past,' he said.

KNOCK. KNOCK. BANG. BANG.

The Angry Freido had now turned his hand into a fist and was banging on the door. The toilet's walls were shuddering.

But Grandad paid no attention. He seemed to be thinking about what Frankie had just said. And then he gave Frankie a nod.

'There's only one way to find out,' Grandad said.

Frankie had not been so relieved since the time his mum told him she'd decided against baking him a Teletubbies-themed cake for his birthday.

BANG. THUMP. THUMP.

'What are you two scoundrels up to in there?' The Amazingly Agitated Freido seemed to be attempting to break the door down with his shoulder.

'Let's go, Grandad,' said Frankie, and put one hand on the old man's shoulder.

Then they both grabbed the handle as Grandad muttered, 'Good luck everybody. *Happy travels!*'

Frankie pressed **ENTER**.

At that exact moment, the toilet door fell off its hinges, and in fell a really, really Angry Freido. '*Now* there is going to be trouble!' he said, as he picked himself up from the stinky toilet floor.

But as the Astonished Freido looked up, he couldn't believe his eyes – because the scoundrels had vanished. Disappeared in a way he could only *dream* of doing.

'What in the name of ...?' he said, completely exasperated.

Clarissa joined him at the doorway. 'Maybe if you learnt that trick,' she said, 'they *would* book you in New York.'

CHAPTER 25

HOME

Dust, wood shavings and pollen. Those were the things Frankie could smell when he woke in his grandad's shed. Frankie turned to see Grandad, who was sitting up and rubbing his eyes.

They looked at each other wordlessly, and then got up and headed out of the shed. Straight away Frankie noticed that Nanna Fish's forget-me-nots and rose bushes were back where they should be. That was a good sign, but Frankie knew it didn't definitely mean that Nanna was back. Maybe his grandad had ended up marrying someone else, who also happened to like flowers. There was only one way to know for sure.

Heart pounding, Frankie walked with his grandad up to the back door of the Fish house.

Grandad put his hand on the doorknob and paused. 'Whatever happens, Frankie, may I say – I have enjoyed spending time with you,' he said quietly. 'Even if we did risk the future of human civilisation.'

'Me too,' Frankie said, with a small, nervous smile.

They both took a big breath as Grandad opened the back door.

Blueberry pancakes and freshly shampooed carpets. That was what Frankie could smell as he stepped inside. A smile crept across his face as he and Grandad walked into the kitchen where they were met with the best sight either of them had ever seen in their entire lives: Nanna Fish, née Nurse Mavis Hopley, standing at the kitchen sink, dunking a teabag into a cup of hot water.

'Honey, you're home!' exclaimed Grandad.

Nanna Fish turned, and with a puzzled smile said, 'Of course I am, you old fool – where else would I be?'

Grandad gave her a big toothy grin followed by a big smooch right on the lips. Frankie was so relieved he didn't even gag. He raced through the house, checking that the bed in his grandparents' room was actually a double bed, that there were flowers in vases in every room, and no dirt on the floor. Even the brown drapes had gone back to Nanna's pretty polka-dotted curtains.

He stood in the lounge looking around as *Family Feud* played on the TV. '*Name something that cannot be changed*,' the host was saying, unaware of how ironic that question was in this particular house.

Everything was exactly the same, Frankie realised, relief rushing through him. Then in the living room, he saw one thing that was different.

On the wall above the couch, the painting of dogs playing poker was gone. A new painting hung in its place. It was a portrait of a young Alfie Fish, moments before the Big Race. Alfie was depicted leaning against his number 42 racing car, talking to an old man and a boy.

'Well, I'll be damned,' said Alfie in amazement, wandering into the room with his arm around Nanna Fish's shoulder.

'It's a wonderful painting, isn't it?' said Nanna. 'I still get goosebumps when I look at it. I've often wondered who that man and young boy are – but I guess we'll never know.'

Frankie and Grandad exchanged a grin.

'Who painted it, Nanna?' asked Frankie.

'Why, your great-uncle Roddy, of course!' said Nanna. 'He always says that the day of the Big Race was when he decided to become a professional artist.' She glanced at the clock. 'Speaking of Roddy, he should be here in an hour or so.'

'Roddy's coming *here*?' asked Grandad, jaw dropping wide.

'Of course, you silly fool! You know he always comes here when he's visiting from Paris,' said Nanna, swatting him fondly. 'And I daresay the two of you will sit around all day, talking about the old days in Glasgow, like you usually do.'

Frankie suddenly felt very warm, and the final little knot of tension in his belly melted away.

The doorbell rang. 'Roddy's plane must have landed early,' Nanna exclaimed, as she bustled off to answer it.

Frankie was feeling so good that at first, he hadn't even noticed who'd entered the living room.

It was only when he felt a hand ruffling his hair that he looked around to see his mum beaming at him.

Behind her was Frankie's dad and Saint Lou, looking thrilled to see him.

'Francis, mate,' said his dad. 'You've grown!'

Grandad smiled and Frankie felt his grin grow wider and wider.

He gave his mum, his dad and even Saint Lou (yes, that's how happy he was to be back) the biggest hugs of their lives.

Tina Fish took her son's face in her hands and examined every inch of it. Her smile dipped just a little. 'Your face ...' she remarked.

Frankie felt the knot quickly reappear. 'What about my face?' he asked, voice quivering slightly.

'You look older somehow,' she said. Then she smiled and gave her son a big squeeze. 'Maybe a little more responsible, too.'

'Well, I guess we all change eventually ... given enough time,' Frankie said, with a wink at his grandad. And Grandad winked back.

CHAPTER 26

AN OFFER NOT EVEN
DREW BIRD
COULD RESIST

A week and a half later, Frankie did something he'd never thought possible.

He turned up to school a whole ten minutes early, because he was desperate to see his best mate Drew Bird.

He ran across the courtyard, through the quadrangle (where some pre-season games of downball were in motion), past the Hedgehog and Miss Merryweather (who were walking hand-in-hand), down to the basketball courts, and onto the oval where the Mosley triplets were already in trouble for throwing dirt at a bird's nest.

Professional teacher's pet Lisa Chadwick and her ponytail flounced by, because of course Lisa Chadwick had to be early on the first day of school.

'Hey Lisa,' Frankie called. 'Have you seen Drew Bird?'

'Fish Guts, do I *look* like I've seen Drew Bird?' she shot back, before walking off briskly like she was on her way to have tea with the Queen.

Frankie rolled his eyes, but then felt a creeping tension all over his body. His parents had stuck to the punishment of not allowing Frankie to see or even speak to Drew during the holidays. For all he knew, the Bird family had moved away. He might never see his best mate again!

But then ...

'**FRANKIE FISH!!!!!**' a voice bellowed out from the adventure playground.

Frankie turned to see a beaming Drew Bird on the swings.

'**FRANKIE FISH! FRANKIE FISH!**'

In a nanosecond, Frankie was at the swings as Drew Bird executed an impressive dismount.

'So apparently we're not allowed to hang out,' said Drew Bird with a big grin. 'Apparently you're a bad influence, Frankie Fish!'

Frankie grinned back and said, 'So are you, Drew Bird! But don't worry, I think I've found a way for us to hang out in secret. What are you like with history?'

THE END
(FOR NOW)

ABOUT THE AUTHOR

Peter Helliar is an Australian comedian, TV presenter and children's author. He lives in Melbourne with his wife and three kids, and currently co-hosts the award-winning news and current-affairs program *The Project* on Network Ten. Helliar plans on being the first human to travel back in time, and expects this to have happened by the time you've read this book.

ACKNOWLEDGEMENTS

To my management team at Token Artists, particularly Kevin Whyte, Dioni Andis, Helen Townshend (who helped me get those early drafts in better shape) and Kathleen McCarthy.

To my *Project* family, especially Craig Campbell, Carrie Bickmore, Waleed Aly and the entire cast and crew who provide such a fun environment to go to work each day.

To the amazing team at Hardie Grant Egmont, who have been a dream to work with, in particular my brilliant editor Marisa Pintado whose guidance and encouragement has made this a much better book. Thanks to you all for the care you've taken with *Frankie Fish*.

To Lesley Vamos, for bringing the characters in my head to life with her incredible illustrations, and designer Kristy Lund-White for a cover I can't stop looking at, and lots of bits and bobs inside too.

To my parents Bill and Helen, whom I choose to call Mum and Dad. Your unwavering support and encouragement over the years has been instrumental in everything I do. To my siblings Mark, Karen and Rachel: growing up in a family that cherishes laughter above almost all else has helped me get to this place right here.

To my brilliant, funny, kind, generous kids, Liam, Aidan and Oscar. This book is for you guys. I am super proud to be your dad.

Finally, to my amazing wife, Brij. Thank you for helping me chase these crazy dreams. Without your patience, understanding, encouragement and love I would get nothing done. Thank you.

Pete

FOR MORE OF FRANKIE AND DREW'S PRANKS, TURN THE PAGE!

IT'S **HILARIOUS,** YOU'LL LOVE IT, JUST ONE MORE PAGE!

NAH, JUST KIDDING, HERE YOU GO!

FRANKIE AND DREW'S TOP TEN PRANKS

1. Turn all the clothes in your sister's wardrobe inside out.

2. Hide whoopee cushions under the couch cushions.

3. At school, pretend to have nits and watch everyone start to scratch.

4. Freeze fake flies into the ice cube tray.

5. Cover your dad's car in Post-It Notes.

6. Put a fake spider in someone's school bag.

7. Glue a coin to the footpath and watch people try to pick it up.

8. Put honey under your mum's car door handles.

9. Fill someone's bag with rocks.

10. Replace the decorations on a cupcake with cough lollies.

THE ACTUAL END